THEM B‍ONES

THEM BONES

HOWARD WALDROP

MARK V. ZIESING
WILLIMANTIC, CONNECTICUT
1989

published by
Mark V. Ziesing
Post Office Box 806
Willimantic, CT 06226

Them Bones copyright ©1984 by Howard Waldrop
Afterword copyright ©1989 by Howard Waldrop
Dustjacket artwork copyright
©1989 by Arnie Fenner and Terry Lee

FIRST HARDCOVER EDITION

Limited Edition ISBN 0-929480-05-8
Trade Edition ISBN 0-929480-04-x
Library of Congress No. 88-051910

For Leigh Kennedy,
who knows what it's like
not to answer the phone for a month.

"Life can only be understood
backward
but it must be lived
forward."

— Kierkegaard

"I often think of
the millions and millions
of the denizens of time
who do not share
the time I live in."

— Claude Ray

"Out of monuments, names,
words, proverbs, traditions,
private records and evidences,
fragments of stories,
passages of books,
and the like,
we do save and recover somewhat
from the Deluge of Time."

— Francis Bacon

"The Past isn't dead.
It ain't even past."

— William Faulkner

"There's a horse in the small mound," said Bessie.

Dr. Kincaid sat behind his camp table in the hot tent, his shirt off, smoking his pipe. The kerosene lamp on the table was turned up too high; its chimney was sooty.

On the Berliner Bijou phonograph, its brass horn only inches from Kincaid's head, Louis Armstrong and His Hot Seven were honking out "Potato Head Blues."

Kincaid, a tall man in his fifties, had been tapping a pencil in time to the music on his field notebook when Bessie walked in. He had only gotten as far as writing "June 17, 1929" across the top of the page. When he listened to music he was oblivious of his surroundings — the heat, mosquitoes, the humidity, the sootiness of the lamp.

Bessie Level waited just inside the netting of the tentflap. She was dressed in jodhpurs, puttees, a khaki shirt and a pith helmet. Kincaid put the pencil inside his notebook, closed and placed it on the folding camp table. A troubled look came across his tanned face. He stood slowly, reached over and flipped the resonator arm up off the spinning Okeh record, turned off the machine. Then he put the record carefully in its buff sleeve, took his pipe from his mouth, pulled on his white shirt and pushed the tails carefully into his canvas hunting pants. He clipped a black bow tie on his collar, pulled on his jaunty L.L. Bean canvas hat and put his pipe back in his mouth. The whole operation was performed with great deliberation.

B
E
S
S
I
E

1

He took two long puffs on his pipe; those and the whisper of the kerosene lamp were the only noises in the tent. Outside, Louisiana swamp sounds drifted in — birds, a bullfrog *chunk*, gleepers, indeterminate mammalian grunts. Kincaid pulled the briar pipe from his mouth.

"That's impossible, Bessie," he said.

"I know," she said, "But it's a horse, it's in the smaller mound, and William found it. He said, 'Miss Bessie, I found a horse.' I said, 'No, William, you didn't,' and he said, 'Yes, ma'am, I did! Come look!' and I did. It's a horse."

"Let's go see it then," said Kincaid. He lifted the chimney and blew out the lamp. They stepped from the darkness of the tent into the darkness of the night.

"I've already sent William for the acetone," said Bessie.

Kincaid's pipe glowed. The night around them was black, broken only by the ghost outline of the workers' tent, the only light on the bluff, on whose walls the shadows of the diggers moved. Lightning bugs dotted the air. Bullfrogs roared off in the bayou. Bessie and Kincaid went down the path from the bluff, which stretched away to either side.

Before them, dimly outlined against the waters of the bayou, were the mounds.

Off to their left, on the old flood terrace of the Suckatoncha Bayou, was a mound, designated as Mound One. It was thirty feet in diameter, ten high. Another time it would have been a promising mound. They would have trenched it first.

Bus as Bessie and Kincaid walked the path from the campsite, they turned to the right, toward the other mound.

It was two mounds, really, 2A and 2B on the surveys. But the mounds were joined by a small ridge running between them, six feet in height. The larger mound, 2A, was what had drawn them there. It was an irregular mound, the base platform some twelve feet high and fifty-five feet in length to the point where it joined the ridge connecting it with the smaller mound. But atop this flat platform of 2A was a conical mound, thirty feet in diameter, whose base was on the platform, and which extended to a curved apex eighteen feet higher.

A platform mound was often an indication of the site of a temple or of a chief's house. A conical mound was often for burial. In two years of digging, Bessie had never seen a

mound so unusual in shape. Neither had Kincaid in his
thirty years of archaeological work.

They had been as excited about it when they arrived at
the site as had the archaeologists on the salvage survey
the year before. To contain themselves, they had begun by
trenching the smaller mound, 2B. They had arrived late
that afternoon, set up camp, and staked the mound areas
off into five-foot grids, with the apex of 2A as the center-
point. Kincaid had quit work, as was his custom, as soon as
the sun set over the bayou.

"I thought you'd stopped work," he said as they stepped
between the stakes toward the smaller mound. The large
mound loomed over them to the northeast, with its ridge of
connecting earth flowing into the base of the smaller.

2B was a conical lump which rose eleven feet from its
base line. It was just over fifteen feet in diameter. On the
side opposite the large mound the ridge of earth tapered
to a point at ground level.

Viewed from the top, 2A and 2B looked like the ornate
fat hour hand of a grandfather clock pointing southwest.

"There was a little light left, so William kept digging.
For the first four feet of the trench, nothing. I've got the
stratigraphy in my field book. Mixed sand and loam, what
you'd expect. A couple of individual earthload impres-
sions, but no containers. We can sift tomorrow, but the
first four feet look pretty sterile to me.

"Then, five feet in, some ash and mica flakes. I had
William widen the trench toward the outside. By then it
was getting pretty dark. While I labeled the mica and was
putting it near the sift box, William found the horse."

They stood at the edge of mound 2B. The test trench
showed as a darker gouge against the grass-covered side
of the mound.

Back up on the bluff, a lantern came around the truck
and tents and started down the pathway.

"Miss Bessie?"

"Down here, William!" she yelled.

Kincaid's pipe turned this way and that in the darkness.
Bessie could tell that he was imagining this spot the way it
was centuries ago. She'd seen him do it on digs the year

before. He'd been at the business so long that he could almost make his imaginings come alive. He had, in classes, when she had been an undergraduate. It had changed her life, made her drop her English major, turn to anthropology, go off to become Dr. Level so that she could return to university and work with him.

She was still new enough at it that what she saw was the silent mounds themselves, as if they had once been living things, and had died here, made to give up their mysteries inch by inch, layer by layer, in a sort of dissection. Sometimes they held no mysteries at all — they were just piles of earth with nothing in them, intended for some purpose never carried out.

She had had a feeling about these mounds when she first saw the survey photographs last winter while they were preparing this summer's salvage. It had been a cool day, and she had imagined digging them in that climate. Now she was here in the middle of a heat wave that made the very air itself seem thick, heavy.

William hurried up with the lantern. He brought the preservation kit — acetone, collodion, varnish, shellac, brushes, picks, gauze, all in a tool box — and set it down.

"Did Miss Bessie tell you what I found?" asked William, an old black man. He was dressed in shapeless clothes and wore shapeless shoes with bunion slits cut in them.

"She says you found us a horse, William," said Kincaid.

"She didn't believe me at first, either, Dr. Kincaid. But my uncle Bodie used to work at a slaughterhouse in Memphis when I was a kid, and I used to watch them dress out everything. I reckon I seen more cow skulls and pig heads than you'll ever see. And horse skulls, too. Ain't no mistaking one, no siree."

"You probably have seen more, William," said Kincaid. His face took on a troubled look again. "Since I deal mostly with a time before the horse was brought back to America."

Kincaid took the lantern and eased sideways into the test trench. He knelt, using a small brush on the dirt of the trench wall.

No one said anything. A mosquito went into Bessie's nose; she snorted and waved her hand in front of her face. The bullfrogs had calmed but the night was full of gleeper sounds. A dog barked far away, over on the Skirville property to the northeast, beyond the barbed wire fence that crossed the old bayou terrace. From there the slow flowing waters turned to trace a course toward the Mississippi River.

Kincaid stepped out of the trench and opened the preservation kit. He picked up a bottle of amber acetone, two one-inch brushes, and an ice pick bent into a curve. He stuck a roll of gauze into his left shirt pocket.

"It's a horse, all right," he said. "I want to go over all the survey notes, and your stratigraphy charts first thing in the morning, Bessie. What time's sunup, William?"

"5:32 A.M., Dr. Kincaid."

"Everybody up at 4:45, eat, and have them leaning on their shovels right here when that sun comes comes up on that bluff."

"Sounds like you want some powerful digging done."

"Before you and the boys are through," said Kincaid, "you might have to dig up this whole parish."

"Yes, sir."

"Get some sleep, William, because none of us might get any for the next week or so."

"I thought we was only going to be here till Thursday, then move on up to Pecania," said William.

"Plans might change," said Kincaid.

"Yes, sir. Holler if you need me, Doctor. Miss Bessie." He went off toward the bluff and the tents.

"You, too, Bessie," said Kincaid. "I hope the first thing we do when we widen this trench tomorrow morning is to find an intrusive burial coming in from the other side. Because what's bothering you right now, and me too, is how a horse got into an undisturbed thirteenth century burial mound."

He turned back to the trench and went in. He puffed on his pipe and began to work, dipping the brush into the acetone, coating the thing in front of him.

"Good night," said Bessie. Kincaid grunted. Bessie

walked up the path, taking care to avoid the grid stakes.

She stood on top of the bluff for a few minutes, watching the lighted trench where Kincaid worked. The lantern cast his shadow up across the face of the larger mound, making it seem to move and jump in the night.

She went back to her tent, closed the netting and took off her clothes without lighting the lamp. There was a mosquito in the tent. She knew it would start to suck her dry as soon as she went to sleep.

After a while, the workers grew quiet in their tents. A dog barked occasionally from the road leading in past the Latouche farmhouse.

Some time later, the moon came up, lighting the campsite and the bluff.

Bessie slept fitfully.

She awoke in the middle of the night. There was a dim light on in Kincaid's tent, which she could see through the mosquito netting. Louis Armstrong was on the phonograph again, still playing "Potato Head Blues" but quietly now, so that only the loud parts carried. Kincaid must have put the soft needle on the tone arm, something he rarely did.

Bessie went back to sleep.

⸻

The sun was almost up. The east was gold and pink where the dawn light hit the bottom of the clouds. Bessie had gotten bacon, eggs, toast, and a mug of terrible chicory coffee from Eli, one of the diggers who was paid two dollars extra a week to cook. She carried the plate and coffee to Kincaid's tent. There was no music playing.

"Knock knock," she said.

"Come in, Bessie! Just the woman I want to see."

"You're especially chipper this morning." She stopped. On the camp table before her was the horse skull, empty eye sockets staring vacantly at her. The skull was covered in varnish and was a dull greasy yellow color.

"Was thin as paper in some places," said Kincaid. "William's a good digger. Tell me what you see here." He pointed to the center of the skull, just above the eyes.

"A hole," she said. She put her breakfast down on a chair, drank a gulp of the peppery coffee.

"Use this pencil," said Kincaid. He handed her a Venus #2. "Unfortunately, you'll find that it goes all the way through and exits near the foramen magnum."

Bessie slid the pencil in the hole carefully, pushed it in. It stopped. She moved the pencil and pushed it until she heard it tap the table.

She examined the hole.

"It doesn't look like it was drilled," she said.

"Go on."

"Couldn't have been a projectile point." She carefully slid the skull to the edge of the table until she could look up from beneath and see the back of the skull and the exit hole. "That would have either shattered the back of the skull or have been shattered itself."

"You're wonderful, Bessie," said Kincaid. Then he handed her a globby nodule of dirt, green and corroded-looking.

"What's that?" she asked. A copper pipestem? That would be something new this far south. Shetrone found some in Ohio last year. Wait. This metal looks too thin to have been cold beaten." She peered at it, end on.

"It's the other end you should be looking at," said Kincaid. He smiled. "I have another, just like it, here. I found them both under the skull while I was working on it. Sorry I couldn't leave them for you to find." He handed her a greenish metal cylinder the size of her little finger.

"We're in trouble if we don't find signs of an intrusion, Bessie. I'm going to call the University and get the head of the survey here anyway. Even if we do figure out some explanation."

Bessie turned the object over. One end hollow, the other closed, with a raised rim on the back. In the center of the rimmed end was a lump.

"I've never seen anything like it," said Bessie. "Either on a dig or in the literature."

"Sure you have, Bessie. You see them every time you go hunting."

She looked down at the horse's skull and the hole

above its eyes. She looked back at the object in her hand again.

"What are we going to do, Bessie?" asked Kincaid. His eyes were serious through the lenses of his glasses.

She realized that what she held in her hand, green, corroded with time, was a brass rifle cartridge.

I'm no Audie Murphy.

So when it was time, I grabbed the reins of the horse, took a deep breath and stepped through the time portal.

There was every chance the horse and I would appear inside a B-25 Mitchell bomber, or a little earlier, a bulldozer or steamroller. Or in the walls of a portable building. They'd assumed that hadn't happened, because they had no record of an explosion that destroyed half of Louisiana during World War II.

What was more likely was that we'd appear just in front of a bulldozer or steamroller or B-25, and be spattered to smithereens when they ran over us.

Ideally where we should come out was on the spot where the airfield *would* be built, sometime in the 1030s or a little earlier.

There was a jerk and a noise as we came through — a lurch like when an elevator just misses a floor and eases back up to it. The horse felt it too, but I had blinders on him.

I *dropped* a couple of inches. So did the horse, and it didn't like it.

I looked around.

Something was very wrong.

Okay, there was no WW II airfield. Good. Better than good.

No construction under way. Better still.

That meant before 1942.

But there was no house off up to the south, nothing but forest and grass. No road. No telephone poles.

To the north there *was* a slope down to where the bayou should be. But the water wasn't there. I could see it through the trees, about a kilometer away.

The bluff extended behind me to the east and west. The sun was bright. A light wind blew through the grass. There

"Study the past if you would divine the future."
— Confucius

was a sound in the air like a waterfall, very far away. The elevation of this whole part of the state isn't more than twenty-five meters. The sound couldn't be a waterfall.

My first job was to secure the area and get out of the way. I threw down the panel marker, pointing northeast, and unlimbered the thirty-cal carbine. A lot of stuff was going to come through the portal in a minute — one hundred forty people, horses, wagons, domestic animals, generators, supplies.

I pulled the horse forward. There were no signs of habitation around. If there were, it would be up to somebody to make excuses. So I don't have to scoop out a foxhole. Or start explaining to CCC people who I was and where I came from, or what the other hundred and forty people were doing coming out of midair.

The waterfall sound became louder and changed from a quiet roar to a different sound, a drumming whir. I looked to the south, where it seemed to be coming from.

At first I thought it was a tornado and that I was a dead man. A cloud was coming toward me out of the bright sky, and coming fast. But it was thin, and it wasn't a cloud. It was a wave of birds, a *tsunami*. I stood transfixed. I had never seen as many birds as this. The column must be a kilometer wide, twenty meters tall. It stretched back out of sight to the southern horizon.

Then the first of them shot overhead, sleek winged shapes — doves? Then more and more, and the flapping became a roar again.

The horse skittered.

The flapping birds were so thick they blotted out the sun. A moving dark shadow covered the clearing and the woods. Thousands of them flew over each second, a couple of hundred meters up. The column stretched southward as far as I could see. Over they went, tiny feathered rockets, moving at a hundred kilometers an hour. They never thinned out enough for the sun to show through.

It started to snow. It looked like snow at first, white flakes that swirled down. Then they hit me and the horse, whose flanks twitched with each tiny impact. It wasn't snow, it was feces. Little warm lumps that came down in a blizzard. The smell was overpowering. I grabbed the reins and pulled the horse toward the shelter of the nearest tree.

What a reception this was going to be for Spaulding and the others. They would step through the portal into semi-darkness and a shit storm. Jesus, the guys who planned this operation never took that into account.

I pulled the horse under the tree. Good thing I hadn't taken the blinders off it. The birds moved overhead, a rippling of dark and lightness against the sky. Their tapered wings pumped and moved, and still the flock stretched north and south without end. The roar was deafening.

I watched them, and patted the horse to reassure it, and kept an eye on the time portal. The others should have already come through. I waited.

And waited and waited.

I couldn't believe it. I'd been there two hours by the watch and no one else had made it. Something was wrong, up there in the future.

The birds were still flying overhead. I'd almost gotten used to the smell and the noise. The ground, the trees, looked like the first flurries of winter had come. Everything was covered with little mottled white and gray lumps.

The birds looked like doves, but they were bluish-brown and had reddish breasts. When I saw that, I realized how very wrong things had gone up there in the future.

I knew there weren't this many birds in the world. A column a kilometer across, twenty meters deep, moving overhead at 100 kph, for two hours. I'm not good at math, but that should be at least a billion.

There aren't that many birds in the world, but there used to be.

I had seen the last passenger pigeon when I was in Washington eight years ago (when there used to be a Washington). Her name was Martha and she was stuffed. She died on September 1, 1914, when so many things were dying, like the Victorian era.

I also remembered something from my Mississippi childhood. On the Natchez Trace Parkway there was a place we sometimes picnicked. It was called Pigeon Roost Creek. A huge area with a shattered forest. Large trees with branches all broken off. A flock of passenger pigeons had roosted there more than a century before. There were so many of them they broke down the trees in a thirty-square-kilometer area.

Those were passenger pigeons overhead. Billions of them. There hadn't been any big flocks for twenty years when Martha, last of her species, died. I remember something about a big hailstorm killing most of the last large flock (after the birds had been hunted and trapped by the millions for a century and a half) in the 1880s.

So this was at most the year 1894.

The Project Scientists had been trying for the 1930s. Off by fifty years, perhaps. But the maps we'd studied said the road, as poor as it was, was built in the 1870s.

Was I as far back as the Civil War era?

And where was everybody? Why hadn't anyone come through the portal? What was wrong?

A moment of existential fear, then it passed.

I'm Madison Yazoo Leake. I was not new at this sort of thing. I was in the Cyprus War ten years ago, in '92. (If you want to call what I did being in a war — interrogating Cypriots in internment camps. I never pulled a trigger, thank god, except on the firing range.)

I was from a bombed-out time in which everybody would eventually die from radiation, from disease, from chemicals. I, we, the Special Group, were on a last-chance attempt to keep the human species of the Earth from dying out completely. We were transported through the magic of unperfected, barely tested, one-way time travel, ostensibly to the past, where we hoped to stop World War III before it started. I was, in effect, a point man. (I was a draftee in the Cyprus War, and *everybody* was a draftee in W W III.)

I still think coming to the past to stop the war involves a

time paradox. I mentioned this the other day to one of the Project Scientists.

"What if we *do* change everything?" I'd asked. "What if there is no war? What if we make it so *you* were never born?"

"What'll you care?" she said. "*You'll* still be alive."

Which, as far as I understood it, was true.

So here I was, covered with passenger pigeon excrement (it brushes off after it dries, but I still needed a bath, fairly soon), waiting for the rest of the Special Group to come through.

The flock overhead was thinning. The sun shone more and more through the whirring pigeon overcast. Then it came out in its glory, and only a few stragglers jetted across its face.

The horse and I were left in a stinking winter wonderland.

I waited for the others to appear in the time gate.

———————

For four days.

Something had gone very, very, *very* wrong. I was alone here. I had enough food for two weeks, but after that I was going to have to go the roots and berries and local wildlife route. And it looked like summer was going here.

I began to view this as a survival exercise which might last the rest of my life.

I was scared.

I'd been as far as a kilometer from the panel marker, to the bayou on the north. Where, on the second day, I had bathed, but washing here is like bathing in Comet cleanser. I had come out wet but gritty.

I'd hobbled the horse and let it graze along the side of the woods, where the sun-hardened pigeon dung hadn't covered everything.

I had never seen so many birds and animals as I had in the last few days. Rabbits, squirrels, quail, deer, field mice. I'd heard something that squealed, and something that coughed, but nothing vaguely human. Birds hopped through the branches of the trees in riotous profusion: bluebirds, cardinals, thrushes, red-winged blackbirds, meadowlarks. Going the nuts and berries and local wildlife route wouldn't be as bad as I had figured.

That left me with a couple of tough questions. Did I stay here and wait for the others, who might never come? Did I try to find other people, find out *when* I was, and get to Baton Rouge? I couldn't change history by myself.

Had the machine malfunctioned and put me down years before the others? Worse yet, years after they had come through? We had an alternate rendezvous point in Baton Rouge. What if there wasn't a Baton Rouge yet?

In the last two cases I'd be on my own, anyway. This whole operation had been carefully planned for everything *except* this. My first job had been to go through and wave off anything coming toward the time portal. I would have had other jobs in the days that followed, but they hadn't figured on me disappearing, or no one else making it across.

I really didn't need this grief. I'd seen enough the last six weeks, up there in 2002, to last me a long, long time.

Find people, that's what I wanted to do.

So I made the decision. I wrote a note and left it on the panel marker. I remembered my pathfinder training, so I would notch all the trees, in case other stragglers like me showed up. The note said I was going to follow Suckatoncha Bayou downstream to the Mississippi River, and then onward to Baton Rouge.

For that was my plan.

On my maps, the Suckatoncha Bayou went north, then east-southeast. Flowed is not the proper word. Most people think bayous are stagnant swamps. They are swampy, but they do flow, slowly. We didn't have a name for them when I was growing up in Mississippi, for they are found nowhere but Louisiana and southern Arkansas. Great flat stretches of water, full of stumps and snags; the confluence of many small creeks and channels, but the land is so flat they spread out for miles.

The Suckatoncha was not where it was supposed to be.

The horse and I went to its margin. Then I mounted up, and we plodded along.

I never liked horses. I still don't. When I was a kid, everybody wanted one. Except me. This one didn't like me, and was too skittish.

When the Special Group decided to go into the past, it chose horsepower over vehicles. (Same reason we were all armed with .30 caliber weapons rather than the standard 7.62 mm rifles. If we'd landed where we should have, the 1930s or '40s, .30-cal ammunition would be much easier to find.) This was backwoods Louisiana, which had barely entered the Bronze Age by 1930. Horses would not have attracted much attention. They could also reproduce themselves and needed no spare parts.

For a few hours we clopped along the mushy ground of the bayou's edge. The bayou extended almost due east. It would empty into the Mississippi, but some kilometers north of where it should, according to the map.

Either my compass was broken, or I was in much worse trouble than I had ever conceived. We'd seen maps all the way back to the French occupation of this area in the late 1600s. The Bayou always flowed east-southeast and emptied into the Mississippi within a couple of kilometers of its (2002 AD) site.

For the last 320 years.

It took a long time for a waterway to change its course by that many kilometers. I must be stranded far, far into the past of this country.

If the group is back here, they're going to have to get ready for a long haul. It won't be just the work of a lifetime changing history. It will be the work of generations. They'll never see to completion what they set in motion. They'll never know.

If they're here somewhere with me.

At sundown, I stopped for the night on a point of high ground (about a meter high). There was a little breeze there, but I knew the mosquitoes (some the size of damsel flies) would come soon. As frogs and other unnamed denizens started an ungodly chorus, I rummaged through my lurp bags for chow.

On the morning of the fifth day I came across a game trail in the pine needles. Since it skirted the margin of the swamp, I followed it.

Out on the waters, alligators the size of culvert pipes were basking in the sun along rotted logs. This morning as I pissed in the water an eight-foot cottonmouth swam by searching for frogs. Last night the noises the frogs made were unbelievable. Most of the animals seemed unafraid, only mildly wary. I thought of having frog legs for supper tonight.

A little while ago I had come upon a huge heron wading near the shore. It began to run, unfolding its wings, and began to lift itself from the water. I thought it would take forever. Then it tucked in its neck, lifted its huge legs, and spread its blue wings on the air. And was gone.

Near noon I came across a footprint on the game path. I stopped the horse. There are people here, at least. I'm not in some dim Holocene past. The print is light and has only the single outline of the sole. So we are dealing with Amerindians, or Cajuns, or a guy in his house slippers.

Now it is my turn to be wary. I speak no Amerindian dialects. (My grandfather was a Choctaw and my great-grandmother a Chickasaw. But they were the Choctaws and Chickasaws who *weren't* removed in the 1800s, the ones who owned slaves and voted and lived in brick houses. I doubted anyone in my family had spoken a native dialect for a century or more. I look Indian, high cheekbones, small hint of epicanthic folds, but I paid little attention to that while growing up. Besides, I doubt Choctaw or Chickasaw would do me any good on this side of the big river.) French? This, after all, is Louisiana. I can't even find a bathroom in French. Some Spanish. If I'm lucky, this is after De Soto's trip through here, and maybe they'll speak some Spanish. My Greek will do me about as much good as tits on a boar shoat. English. There's always English. Gestures? I never studied either Amerindian or American Sign Language.

Maybe this is just a guy in his house shoes. Maybe I'm

not stranded in some unthinkable past. Maybe when I go to the river there'll be steamboats and riverboat gamblers and telephones and cars.

Not a chance, with the bayou running straight east as an arrow into the Mississippi River.

Madison Yazoo Leake, you are on your own.

———

It was later and I was bathing in a creek which came out of the pines and emptied into the bayou. I had been following the footprints for a couple of hours and they looked no fresher to me. It was warm and muggy.

I had no liking for the snakes and alligators, or the silty waters of the bayou. So when I found this clear water, I was ready to clean up. The water was only half a meter deep and a meter across where I bathed. The water was cool, refreshing. I had cleaned every orifice twice. I had soaped and rinsed and now I was soaking, watching my belly hairs float.

The horse whinnied.

I turned.

They stood watching me: Larry, Curly, and Moe.

Except that these three were nearly naked. They wore breechcloths. They had bows, arrows, spears and clubs. They had feathers in their hair and pearls around their necks.

My heart stopped.

"Nah Sue Day Ho," said Moe.

He really didn't look much like Moe, except that his hair hung in bangs on the front and he had a small pot belly and bandy legs. Larry didn't look much like Larry, except that his hair was pulled up into two long knots, one over each ear, his nose was large and he was the skinniest of the three.

Curly looked just like Curly. He was stout, built like a gorilla, and his head was shaved. He was tattooed all over — round circles, bands of blue and green. A swastika curved over his navel.

All three wore ornaments the size of teacups in their earlobes.

"Nah Sue Day Ho," Moe repeated.

My first impression was going away. There were three Amerindians here, and they were armed. Each had a couple of rabbits and some squirrels tied to their loincloths with rawhide thongs.

"Nah Sue Day Ho," Moe said. I didn't know if it was a question, a greeting, a warning. Their faces were impassive. A very unfunny Dr. Howard, Dr. Fine, Dr. Howard.

"Hello," I said and held up my right hand in greeting, palm out. That was supposed to be universal. As I did so I slid up out of the water and stood, my left hand finding the buttplate of the carbine.

As I stood, their eyes widened a little and they looked at my crotch. I resisted the temptation to look down. It was probably an old trick.

"Hello," I said again, then, "Friend." I didn't know whether I wanted to be friends with them or not. I just didn't want a fight. I was ashamed of myself for letting them walk right up on me.

"Cue Way No Hay?" asked Moe. His eyes went to my crotch again, then back to my face. "Ho Gway din Now."

"¡Amigos!" I said. "¿Como se llama?"

"Cue Way No Hay?" Moe asked, his face twisting. Curly held a big war club with a ball and a single big spike on the end of it. I'd seen clubs like that in the paintings of Thomas Hart Benton.

The horse made another rude noise. The three jumped, then looked over at it. I felt better about myself then. It must have been behind the bushes when they came up, and they hadn't seen it. Their eyes really got wide then. They turned to face it. They made noises among themselves.

I pulled the carbine up with my left hand (I'm a lefty) while keeping my right hand up and open.

"Bu Show Mo Toy?" asked Moe.

"Condo Ku Moy no-hat?" asked Curly.

"Moy Doe!" said Larry, hefting his spear and looking toward the horse.

The horse stamped turf into the air. It was upset.

"Cue Way No Hay?" asked Moe again. "Cue-Way-

No-Hay?" he asked slowly, as if repeating it for a child.

Larry was the one I was worried about. He was going to do something about the horse soon. I was afraid he was going to spear it.

"*Amigos,*" I said. "Friends. Hello." My mind wasn't working at all.

Curly moved back from the horse. He said something to Moe.

I had to do something.

I fired the carbine once, into the air.

I don't know what reaction I expected: fear, wonderment, anger. It wasn't what I got.

"Ah Muy nu-ho," said Moe, shrugging his shoulders. He made a deprecatory gesture with his hands, as if giving up on me.

The horse tried to pull away from the tree I'd tied it to. The eyes of the horse rolled a little. Who was afraid of a horse but not a gun?

I looked toward the horse.

When I turned back, the men were gone. One of the nearby bushes still swayed a little where they had brushed it on their way past.

"Hey, wait!" I yelled.

My hand started to shake. I had been holding it up in the air the whole time.

I followed their tracks. They joined others on a footpath. I rode slowly. I don't think I really wanted to catch up with them. It was late afternoon. I neared the Mississippi.

I saw the village long before I got near it. The trees thinned out. Then there was a cleared area, which had been slashed-and-burned, half a kilometer across. Beyond that were the fields, stretching a kilometer in three directions. Their village lay beyond the fields.

It was palisaded, surrounded by an earthen embankment higher than the surrounding fields. The Mississippi River lay back of it. I could see two high places within the town walls — one had a building atop it, and there were statues of some kind on the roof. I counted housetops, rounded, mud-covered things. There were at least fifty inside the part of the walls I could see.

At the near edge of the fields were two huge mounds of dirt. Ten meters high, twenty in diameter. They were scraped bare and had nothing growing on them.

The fields were full of various kinds of beans, squash, pumpkins, and gourds. It was late in the season. Tendrils of climbing beans hung in the air on sun-bleached cane poles. Row on row of short cornstalks with small ears on them grew as far as I could see to the right. Their leaves were beginning to curl and turn yellow. It must be September here.

There should have been people in sight, but there was no one. I thought maybe they had all run away. Then I saw that the walls, which must have ramparts inside, bristled with spears. At the log notches, more than two hundred people watched me, unmoving.

Then I saw the fields weren't entirely deserted. Someone sat on a stump, working at something in his hand. Whittling, maybe. The stump was next to the path through the fields, surrounded by pepper plants.

I rode within thirty meters of him, then dismounted and tied the horse to another stump. I eased the safety off the carbine and kept an eye on the village. They just stared back, unmoving.

I walked toward the man, held up my hand. Wind rustled through the corn. He stopped what he was doing. He had some kind of stone in his hand and was carving on it with a piece of metal.

He was unarmed. He had on a red- and white-striped loincloth and wore a pair of moccasins. His hair was black, pulled back in two braids, and had a single feather in it. He had one small pearl in his left ear. He was much more confidence-inspiring than the three who had surprised me at the spring.

I stopped. He regarded me calmly. His skin was an even copper color, like an old penny. He had no tattoos.

His eyes went to the horse tethered far away. Then he studied me, my carbine, my clothes.

My arm was still up in greeting.

"Hello," I said. "*Amigo.* Friend."
"Hello," he said, in Greek.

the box

1

DA FORM 1   1432 Z 01 OCT 2002

COMP ___147___   TOE ___148___

PRES FOR DUTY: 146

MISSING LINE OF DUTY   1

TOTAL: 147

FOR: S. SPAULDING   BY: BARNES, BONNIE

COL, INF.   CPT ADC

COMMANDING   ADJUTANT

AFP 907-11M-996

Smith's Diary   Oct 4

Forty-five minutes later Sgt. Croft came out of the portal behind me.

And so on through the night, the next day and night, and early into the second morning.

One hundred and forty-six of us.

There is still no sign of Leake, or of what happened to him. Dr. Heidegger thought the jump-reading on the instruments just before Leake went through may have something to do with it. The point man could be back where we started from, a few days before or after where we started from, Up There.

If he is, he knows where he is better than we do. Or when, for that matter. Colonel Spaulding sent scouts out on two-hour rides in every direction. All they found were trails, but nothing else manmade, so far. No smoke, no footprints, no boats, no houses, no aircraft.

We have set up camp on the bluff overlooking the bayou. It's the highest point for kilometers around. Spaulding had us dig in the usual star pattern defenses, but hasn't let us set up anything permanent yet.

Everybody's getting this wild look in their eyes, if they didn't already have it before we left Up There. This is it, whenever and wherever it is. We're stuck here, unless life somehow goes on Up There, and they find some way to come get us. We knew that when we came through, but we also thought we'd be somewhere in the neighborhood of eighty years from the time we started.

Spaulding is taking it right, acting like this is just another exercise, some problem the War College has set for him. What did we expect from a thirty-year man? Come to think of it, what's a 'copter pilot like me doing here, anyway? As acting assistant adjutant, no less.

It's better than being back Up There, dying with the rest of them.

Acting assistant adjutant, I can see giving the CIA spooks orders some day when everybody else is out of the camp. They all have shifty eyes and look like insurance agents on an overnight campout. Jeez.

There are more lightning bugs and bigger mosquitoes here than I ever imagined could live in Louisiana.

And so, as Pepys used to say, to bed.

They looked like a bunch of ants. They were doing several things at once with a minimum of frenzy. Picks and shovels rose, fell, ladled. Two workers were tossing dirt in the air over a fine wire mesh screen. Only Kincaid's shoes and elbows showed out of the test trench.

Bessie coated the second horse's skull with shellac. It had no bullet holes in it. There was such a tangle of bones in the mound that it was impossible to leave the topmost *in situ* and still find out anything. Bones of horses, all in a twisted pile, five, six, maybe more complete skeletons.

Bessie looked up at the large double mound with its row of stakes. A small shiver went through her. She rubbed her arms. The air was hot and blue, with no seeming promise of rain.

The Suckatoncha Bayou was gray and flat through the brush. In the great flood of two years ago, thirty people had been drowned by its waters. Livestock, bloated and ruptured, had floated in it for weeks. Whole houses had been found fifty miles from their pilings. Water had come halfway up the bluff.

Under Huey "Kingfish" Long, the state had set up the Suckatoncha Bayou Relief Project, a series of dams to hold back future floods. The first of the dams was ten miles away, and the land around the bayou was to be slowly covered during the next two years.

The state Salvage Survey had mapped those archeological sites which would be flooded (and found a few new ones in the process). Now Bessie, Kincaid and five other teams were digging along the edges of the Bayou, trying to learn what they could before the waters covered them forever.

The Salvage Project had started with the understanding that there were three months left before the first of the mounds would be covered. That had been before spring rains caused the state water people to shut the dams ahead of schedule. The spillways ten miles up weren't

BESSIE

2

completed yet, so they had shut some farther downstream, starting the waters creeping upward.

Time and rain were the enemies now. If rainy weather set in, the waters would rise at a tremendous rate in a few days. They would also stop or slow down work on all the digs at the same time. All the salvage crews' time would be spent trying to keep the opened mounds and village sites dry and intact.

There was a chance of rain that afternoon, the usual southern evening thunderstorms. The air was humid and thick though as yet there wasn't a cloud in the sky.

Early morning had been no less busy. Kincaid had driven to Suckatoncha, used the town marshal's telephone, and called the University. He'd talked to the Project Director and laid it on the line. He wanted to pull in two other teams, plus the office staff, photographers, artists, and curators, to the site.

That had been on the basis of the first equine skull.

While he was in town, Bessie had taken the second out of the test trench. Now Kincaid was back, submerged in the dig.

William brought her a few potsherds with Kincaid's ink-scribbled location numerals on them. She recognized them immediately; Coles Creek red, white, and black rims. That would normally mean somewhere between 700 and 1500 A.D. No surprise there, except the upper date. That might explain the horses — not really, though. The first hadn't been on the continent until the second or third decade, none known in this area until De Soto's march north of here in 1540.

It was possible this segment of the Coles Creek culture could have lasted a few more decades, maybe until the middle of the century, still been viable when the Spanish came through.

What about the cartridge, though?

That was no Spanish musket ball, no arquebus load. Most of the conquistadors depended on crossbows for their main armaments until the mid-1500s anyway. Usually they only had ten or twelve firearms, plus a few small cannon, for each hundred soldiers. This was a modern brass cartridge.

There must be a modern intrusion. The soil was layered and undisturbed on each side of the test cut. They had cut a second trench in from the other end. It would meet the first trench slightly off center of the mound.

So far the soil there too was undisturbed, evenly layered, as Kincaid had said in his last note brought in with the shards.

Bessie left the sorting tent and went down the bluff to the dig. She stepped into the trench behind Kincaid. All she could see of him was his back.

"How are the potsherds?" she asked.

"If this is a hoax," he said, dusting away with a small paint brush, "it's a good one. Come down here."

Bessie wedged herself down in the trench beside him. The smell of drying earth filled her nose, surrounded her, got in her clothes. She let her eyes go up from the floor of the trench, paved with horse bones, to where Kincaid pointed.

Embedded in the dirt, above the bones and skulls, were grave goods — weapons, pots, black mold where the wooden handles of axes had been. Each was broken, in one place on the projectile points, with a single hole through the clay pots, making them useless in everyday life.

But not the life beyond. The people who had made these mounds had broken the objects they placed in the graves with their dead, killing them as dead as the persons or animals buried there.

Bessie stood up. She brushed her hands on her jodhpurs, straightened a marker stick on the trench lip. Kincaid stood up too.

"William! Washington?"

The two men put down their work and came over.

"Yassuh?"

"Put the number-two tarp over this mound, will you. Put spike markers in all the stick holes, but leave it just like it is. Maybe a support in the center of the trench. Stop the digging here. I want it just like this when the Director gets here."

"Can do," said William. "What about the other test trench?"

"More horses?"

"Two or three, maybe more."

"Grave goods?"

"Yessir."

"What I expected. I knew you would have called if you found anything else unusual. We'll finish this one as soon as the others get here."

"Once I got used to finding them horses, I was okay," said William. He wiped his hands across the stocking he wore over his hair while digging.

"This is going to turn into a major dig. How are we for food?"

"Fine for us. How many people coming?"

"The other crews will have their own supplies. The office staff will come. I think they'll bring the big tent."

"We can stretch it, I guess," said William. "We have to reprovision the end of next week anyway. Might have to move it up a few days."

"Well, let me know when the mound is secure. We can figure out what to do from there."

Bessie walked beside Kincaid up the bluff to the sorting tent and sat down at the table. The first horse skull with the bullet hole in it stared at them like a three-eyed monster.

"It's not like you not to talk," said Kincaid, taking off his hat and lighting his pipe.

"Well, this is where our reputations go on the line, isn't it?" she asked. "I mean, there could be some explanation that makes some sense."

"I can see it now," said Kincaid, smiling. "Someone dug a hole, filled it with dead horses, shot them with a new rifle, put the cartridges in the pit, filled it up to the level of the horses, put in Coles Creek grave goods, finished off the mound and planted a tree on top of it.

"And they did all this at least sixty years ago, when the first metal cartridges came into general use, so they could pull a good one on some poor damn fool university professors in the year of the Lord 1929.

"That's the obvious explanation," he finished.

"Are we going to leave it like this until the Director gets here?"

"Mound 2B anyway. As soon as William gets the tarp on, and I finish my pipe, let's go start trenching 2A."

Bessie walked to the open tent flap, watched the men covering as much of the small mound as they could. She heard the snick of Kincaid's match, the puff of his pipe.

He was staring into the eyeholes of the horse skull as if they could tell him something.

She looked back at the large mound, which loomed over the other like a small fort. Her knees shook.

"Damn," she said quietly.

Kincaid looked at her through his thick glasses. "Ditto," he said.

They were trying to feed my horse meat.

The man's name, he said, was Took-His-Time, because of the extraordinary pains his mother had when he was born.

I asked him where he had learned to speak Greek. He said that when he was a boy, some mean Traders had taken him away from his people and made him interpret for them. He had escaped, but still spoke Greek because the Traders now, much nicer ones, still came back each year to do business.

**L
E
A
K
E

2**

He asked if I was a Trader or a Northerner.

"No."

"We didn't think so" — he indicated the crowd who had come out of the stockaded village — "because your dong isn't whacked."

I blushed.

"All our men are," said Took-His-Time. "So are the Northerners and the Traders, even though their customs are nothing like ours."

"Uh, where am I?"

"Right here," said Took-His-Time.

"No. I mean, what is that river?"

"Mes-A-Sepa," he said. "That means Big River. That's what we call it."

I watched the skittish crowd putting down clay dishes of meat a few meters from my tethered horse. It was getting nervous.

"Could you tell them it eats grass?" I said.

He looked at me with his dark eyes a moment, then said something in his own language. They looked at him, then some of them ran back inside the walls.

"They think it's a big dog," he said. "What is it?"

> "Time will bring to light whatever is hidden; it will conceal and cover up what is now shining with the greatest splendor."
> — Horace

"A horse," I said.

"Ah," he said, looking at it a moment. "So that's what they look like! I always thought they had wings."

"You know what they are?"

"I know of them, the name," he said. "Sometimes it was all the Traders talked about among themselves. All the time they talked of their homes across the sea, and their horses. But I've never seen one. They run fast?"

"This one doesn't," I said. "Would you like to touch it?"

"Looks dangerous to me," he said. He said something in the other language. I noticed a subtle change in six or seven of the guys with spears and clubs. They began to watch me instead of the horse.

"I have to ask you this, old custom," said Took-His-Time. "Do you mean us any harm, or are you a thief?"

"Huh? No, I don't want to hurt anybody. I'm lost."

Took-His-Time said something to the others. They smiled and turned back to watching the horse.

"If you're lost, can we help you find the way?"

"I hope so. Have you seen any others like me?"

"Guys with their dongs not whacked riding horses? I'm sure you're the first."

"Some of them might be women. But they'd be riding, too."

"That would scare the average guy to death," said Took-His-Time.

Somebody rolled the horse a cabbage-looking thing. It reached its neck out and began to nibble at the leaves.

"Ooooh," said the crowd.

"Have you fallen down recently, or anything like that? Excuse me," said Took-His-Time. "I forgot to ask your name."

"Madison Yazoo Leake," I said.

"Yazoo is a name I can say," he said. "Well, Yazoo, would you like to come to my house for supper?"

"Will the horse be all right?"

"I guarantee *nobody's* going to touch it," he said.

He took me to his wattle and lath hut, which looked just like all the others. A very pretty woman, about eight months pregnant, was cooking inside.

"This is Sunflower, my wife," he said. "We are going to have a child soon." He said something to her, she answered him, and smiled. There was a pot cooking. In it was a stew, corn, beans, and meat of some kind. The pot wasn't over the fire. Round clay balls, glowing red-hot, were heaped in the coals. Occasionally Sunflower would lift one and drop it into the stew. Soon it was boiling. It smelled wonderful.

The room was dark, covered with skins. Around the corners were various kinds of stone, sticks, carvings of some sort. I looked at one. It was a small raccoon with a fish in its paws — you could see each band of the raccoon's tail, every scale of the fish.

Took-His-Time picked it up. "Not very good," he said. "Now, my dead uncle, he could *really* carve a pipe."

"Is that what you do?"

"Carve pipes? Yes" — he looked down at the floor — "they say I do."

"These are nice," I said.

He smiled and said something to Sunflower. She looked at me and smiled, then laughed.

"Supper will be a little while," he said. "Would you like a walk around the town? Perhaps it will help you remember your way."

"Sure," I said.

The village, which overlooked the fields and the river, was laid out around a central plaza. On each end of the plaza was a large mound. On the rounded one was a hut, just a little bigger than the others. Opposite it across the hardpacked plaza was another mound, like a flat-topped pyramid. On top of it was a long low building made of big trees. On each end and in the middle was the carved effigy of a big crested bird with a long beak.

"That's our temple," said Took-His-Time. "Not much, but we like it."

"Who lives over there?" I asked, pointing across the plaza.

"Well, if we stay around a few more minutes, you'd see. That's where Sun Man lives. He's the chief. Every morning he yells the sun up, and he cries out in anguish every night when it goes down. All the Sun Men do that."

"How many are there?"

"Oh, every town has one. Thousands, I guess, maybe more. We belong to this confederacy, most of it's on the other side of the River. To the west, that's where the Huastecas, the Meshicas, live. They speak a language in which their god's name sounds like a bird fart. They're mean people, but we trade with them and have a few ritual wars."

"What do your people do most of the time?"

"Hunt. Fish. Raise crops. I make pipes, others tan hides, make spears, stuff like that. We trade with other Sun Villages. Bury folks, raise kids, the usual things."

"And trade with these Traders and Northerners?"

"Once a year or so. You missed them. Have to wait till the spring, just before the crops, before you can see them. We spend most of our winter making geejaws and doodads. They trade us cloth, axes, knives, beads, things we're too lazy to learn how to make ourselves."

There was a group of people near one of the larger huts north of the plaza. Most of them, men and women, were tattooed heavily with weird designs. Like the ones on the three guys I'd seen in the afternoon.

In fact, Moe and Curly were in the group. Curly waved to Took-His-Time.

"That's one of the hunters I saw this afternoon," I said.

Another guy turned to stare at me. His face was a green design of lightning bolts and tears. A third weeping eye was tattooed on his forehead. He wore bear's teeth earrings. His hands had outlines of hands incised on them, smaller and smaller in infinite regress.

"Those are the Buzzard Cult people," said Took-His-Time, not looking at the man who stared back. "The man looking at you is Hamboon Bokulla, which means Dreaming Killer. He is their leader."

"Buzzard Cult?"

"Our people, the Sun People, take death as it comes. We bury our dead in big piles of dirt, and put nice things in with them in death. But the Buzzard Cult people are something new. They worship Death itself, mourning, weeping, decay. All those hand and eye things. They don't worship the Woodpecker." He nodded toward the temple.

"But they're still part of our village," he said. "They've sprung up everywhere. They think the world is going to end soon, and they dance a little dance to help it along."

"What do you believe?"

"I believe supper's ready."

That's how it started. That's how I'm living in this village of two hundred huts on the Mississippi River, with people who worship a woodpecker, and who bury their dead in mounds.

I didn't mean to end up living here, but it happened. I was conscientious. I was trying to find out where and when I was, and nobody seemed to know.

I moved the horse in near the plaza on my second day there. People piled food around it, and stood talking about it for hours.

In those first few days I checked my radio beacon locator every few hours to see if anything has happened at the time portal. Took-His-Time introduced me to Sun Man, a nice old thin guy, and his nephew, who is likely to be the next Sun Man. (When a Sun Man dies, all the women get together and choose a new one. The closest kin a new Sun Man can be to the old one is on the old Sun Man's sister's side.) I tried to find out what I could, which is the stuff everybody seems to know — how many Sun Villages there are, how long the River is, when the crops should be planted, the best places to fish, how to make babies. For all this, Took-His-Time, patient as his name, acted as interpreter. I was picking up a few words and phrases from him, and from Sunflower ("kick," for instance).

The village is called the Village, the river is the River, the sky the Sky, and the people the People. The third day I was there, Took and Sunflower had a conference, and asked me if I'd like to stay as a guest until I found the people I was looking for.

I said yes. I began to help Sunflower around the hut, went on walks with Took, tried to see how he made pipes. I learned words and looked after the horse.

At first, I oiled my rifle every night, and kept my knife sharp. I checked the beacon every few hours, then once a day, every two days.

I put the carbine into an oiled skin, put it behind my place in the hut. I washed my fatigues in the River, learned the local customs. (On the second day, I'd asked Took about certain functions. He pointed outside the village to a bank leading down to the River. "That's called Shit Hill," he said. "Watch your step up there. Piss anywhere past the crop lines.")

So here I am, learning about pipestone. Sunflower just made me a breechcloth. I felt silly, but took off my fatigues (behind a skin frame) and bundled them away with my military gear.

I modeled the loincloth for them.

Sunflower said something. "What?" I asked.

"She says you'd never know your dong wasn't whacked."

I smiled, I blushed.

"Thank you, Sunflower," I said.

the box

2

Smith's Diary   Oct 8

We have music now, if you can call it that.

Specialist Jones, against orders, brought his portable minicassette deck, and what he thought were twenty of his best tapes. He'd stashed it in his combat gear.

Only before he left, somebody went through his stuff, took all the music he'd picked, and left him with three tapes.

They are: Great Movie Love Themes *sung by Roger Whitaker,* 16 Hits *by Glenn Miller and* Rip My Duck *by Moe and the Meanies. That's about as eclectic as you can get.*

We know all this because Specialist Jones brought the deck to us on the sixth day of our exile. He wasn't the only one who noticed people going out of their minds from boredom. He volunteered his music for morale.

Sergeant Sigmo, the commo NCO, rigged it to the PA and alarm system. From 1400 to dusk every day, we have music.

The Miller tape is getting the most wear. Moe and the Meanies drive you right up the tent walls in thirty seconds, but then, that was their stated aim. I've seen people jokingly ease the safety catches off their carbines every time Roger Whitaker comes on. It beats staring at the bayou, or filling sandbags, or feeding the horses, or whatever else there is to do while we wait for the scouts.

━━━━━━━━━

Spaulding just called an officer's meeting. The recon from the north just returned.

Call him Ishmael.

We had gone down to the edge of the River to see what was there. The day was warm and the sun was bright, though by my reckoning it should be late November.

Took had a fishing spear with him. Mounted on the shaft were three copper prongs. A rawhide thong passed through the head, through the shaft and onto a coil tied around his waist.

He walked to the sandbar's edge and studied the water, shading his eyes against the sun.

Something large was moving under the water down the bank.

"What's that?" I asked. I thought it might be an alligator. Took turned, saw what I pointed at. He grabbed my arm, squeezed it in a sign for me to be quiet. He held out his hand for my javelin. I gave it to him.

He walked slowly back off the the sandbar, then turned into the grass alongside the River. I stayed where I was. I couldn't see him fro a few minutes, but knew he was moving slowly through the tall grass. I saw a few fronds bend.

Whatever the thing was, it disappeared underwater from time to time, surfacing nearer or farther from the bank. I still couldn't tell what it was. It looked like a dark lump in the shadows from the overhanging trees.

I didn't see Took until his fishing spear shot out on its thong from the last of the grass. It flashed in the water.

A ton of foam shot into the air.

L
E
A
K
E

3

"The *Indians* call this watry Waggon
Canoo, a Vessel none can brag on;
Cut from a *Popular-Tree*, or *Pine*
And Fashion'd like a Trough for Swine"
— Ebenezer Cooke

"Hoo-eee! Hoo-eee!" yelled Took. The thong stretched tight. The spear shaft went cartwheeling up the rawhide and slammed into the trees overhead.

"Yaz!" he yelled.

Other men were already running out of the village and the fields.

As I ran toward him I saw my javelin arc out into the frothing water. A huge coughing noise came from the River. As I ran through the grass I saw other large dark shapes, which I had not seen before, disappearing downriver.

Some of the guys got there before I did. They threw their spears out. The water turned red and quit splashing before I got there.

Others jumped into canoes at the landing, yelling, paddling toward where the other dark shapes had gone.

I reached Took and grabbed the thong he was holding. Someone came over in a canoe, dropped a rope down into the bloody water, then threw the end to us. We heaved and hoed.

I don't know what I was expecting, but it wasn't this.

First came a flat forked tail, then wrinkled mounds of pink skin, then flippers with spears in them, and last, something like the head of a walrus without the tusks. The damn thing must have weighed half a metric ton.

Its face was covered with bristles the size of No. 2 pencils.

It was a manatee, the largest I'd ever seen. In the time I came from, they were nearly extinct. They were always (before the War) getting run over by assholes in speedboats, or shot by kids with .22s, or something. Once there had been huge numbers of them in the rivers of the South.

Well, they're still *here*. A couple of the canoes had harpooned one, and there was shouting all up and down the River as the rest of them got away.

There was general happiness all around. A ton of meat was a ton of meat. They began to dress out the two manatees on the shore.

I went around to the head of the one Took had harpooned. It still had a water lily hanging out of one side of its wide flat mouth.

The whole village was ecstatic.

This is a place for boys and girls who never grew up.

While they were waiting, the first of the trucks drove up.
The crew led by Dr. Jameson arrived just after noon.
Bessie and Kincaid had gone up to check the survey and
the preliminary stakedown on the larger mound, and
planned the trench to take them a few feet off center, from
ten feet out to twenty feet beyond the mound.

Jameson looked at the horse skulls and
the cartridges, then without a word went down
to the trench in the smaller mound and
crawled under the tarp to have a look for
himself.

He came back wiping sweat.

"I couldn't see any goddamn intrusions,"
he said to Kincaid. "Uh, pardon me, Bessie."
His sunburned face went redder. He was just
over forty, already stoop-shouldered from
crawling around digs with no headroom in
them.

He was dressed in dark brown jodhpurs, a
khaki shirt and an old Marine campaign hat.
Bessie knew that his role model (from the
field of paleontology, not an archeologist at
all) was Roy Chapman Andrews, whose spec-
tacular find of dinosaur eggs in the Gobi
Desert of Mongolia was the biggest news
since Carter opened Tut's tomb in '26.

Jameson had eyes the color of the dust he
was always covered with.

"It's possible we're dealing with two things
here," he said, taking off his hat, spinning it
and catching it repeatedly as he talked.

B
E
S
S
I
E

3

"One, a post-Columbus survival of the culture, entirely
possible, combined with a Spanish incident, perhaps de
Soto, perhaps as late as the French. That would be rare
enough itself.

"And, two, an intrusive cartridge burial." He stopped.

"Don't say it. Someone shot a bunch of rounds into the
mound, one of which just happened to hit one of the
equines. Then the spent cartridges worked themselves
down to that level in a few years." He looked at them.

"It's a hoax," he said. He looked at them a minute more, while they said nothing. On the desk before him were the skulls, cartridges, potsherds and field notes.

"I need a drink," he said finally, and sat down on a camp stool.

"It'll have to be lemonade or water," said Bessie. "I don't think Washington made a run to the bootlegger this week yet."

"Well, I did," said Jameson. He disappeared out of the tentflap, returning a moment later with a hip flask. He offered them a drink, which they refused.

He looked over the field notes again. "Goddamn Coles Creek rolled rim potsherds," he said. "I've seen enough in the last two weeks to keep me the rest of my life. I sometimes think all those people did was sleep, eat, bury their dead, and make pots."

"Well, it's good that they did," said Kincaid, "or we'd all be out of jobs."

"Gillihan at least got that rock shelter down by the river," said Jameson. "He was real pis— very upset that you wanted him pulled out of it. He's got the students with him, of course, and this is the best shelter we've ever seen. It had some big cat bones with it."

"Well, the real question is," said Kincaid, "do we start on the mound trench now, or do we wait for the Director?"

"I don't want my shovels to cool off," said Jameson.

"Bessie?"

"Let's do it. Only thing is, we're going to have to answer some questions all over again when Gillihan gets here."

"We'll leave a note on the tent telling them to look over this stuff *before* they come down."

"By the way," said Jameson, "you know it's been raining up north for two days straight now?"

the box

3

Smith's Diary   Oct 13

The second day at the old airfield, which will someday sit right up there on the bluff, Spaulding noticed that one of the men had an old Dalmatian (which he was of course calling Sparky) with him.

The soldier said he'd found him when we arrived, and that the vet needed to look it over, if that was okay.

Spaulding told him yes, but not to become too attached to it, as there was no way he could keep it on the mission.

The vet looked Sparky over, kenneled him, as the dog was all banged up and emaciated. Every day the soldier came to talk to Sparky and play with him.

Then Heidegger got here a week later, and started sending the mice back, then the monkeys, calibrating the portal. How he kept track of the comings and goings, I don't know. Heidegger's so far out of it nobody could talk to him.

Anyway, Heidegger needs something to really calibrate the machine, looks around and sees Sparky over in the vet's office. What does he know? So one night he takes Sparky and puts him into the machine.

Sparky knew something was up, tries to chew Heidegger's arms off (I don't blame him). Heidegger wrestles him into the machine. Sparky goes wild, throws himself into the walls, hurts himself. Heidegger throws the switch.

Five days earlier, or whatever, Sparky hadn't shown up.

Heidegger's blown it (since Sparky was over there in the cage, Heidegger didn't know what he was waiting for). After Heidegger sent the dog back, the soldier shows up to play with Sparky. Sparky's gone. Where's my dog? he asks. The vet doesn't know. They go to Spaulding. Spaulding goes to Heidegger.

"Lost, I guess," says Heidegger. "I'm sorry I lost your animal. I thought it was for the experiments. And I'm sorry I hurt it."

"Hurt him? Just what the hell did you do?" asked the soldier, crying.

"While he was trying to bite me, he hung his dewclaw on the machine and tore it. There was some blood. I'm sorry."

"Thanks a whole fucking lot," said the soldier. "I'm going to kill you someday."

The vet jumped in and calmed the soldier down. When he left, the vet turned to Heidegger.

"Wherever Sparky is," said the vet, "he won't have any more dewclaws to hang things up on."

"What do you mean?" asked Heidegger.

"Well, I took one of his dewclaws off, myself, when the soldier brought him in the first time. It was barely attached and infected."

Heidegger looked him squarely in the eyes.

"Which dewclaw was that?" he asked.

"The left one. He only had the right one when you handled him."

Heidegger took off his glasses and rubbed his eyes. "The dog had two dewclaws when I put him in the machine. And," he said, turning back to the machine and looking at it with a new respect, "it was the left dewclaw which hung up on the wall and tore before I sent the dog back."

———————

Spaulding said that's when Heidegger knew it would all work, and that's when we should have been worried.

———————

It takes all kinds.

Sunflower was in labor and there was a hell of a storm coming.

We just don't have weather like that in the time I come from. The sky had clouded up late in the afternoon. A huge black thunderhead covered the whole southern sky by dusk. The top of it flashed silver and purple with lightning even before the sunlight faded. It must have been forty kilometers away when it formed. It was moving slowly and majestically toward us.

L E A K E 4

We were hearing the thunder by the time the midwife came and shooed us out. A flash of lightning made the sky white. Torches were lit down at the plaza.

"What's up?" I asked Took-His-Time.

"People are going to pray to the Woodpecker God," said Took. "Lightning tends to hit the village."

"Oh? Should we go down there?"

"I can pray just as good here. Sun Man's in fine form without me."

There was a high moan from Sunflower in the hut.

"Let's get a little farther away," said Took.

"Are you worried? I am," I said.

"It's in the beak of the God," said Took. "Tradition says I shouldn't be in earshot, though, or he may be born deaf."

We walked farther toward the plaza. Some of the Buzzard Cult people were standing in the doorway of a hut, looking toward the storm, not moving, not saying anything.

The thunder came in a continuous rumble, the cloud a constant pulse of lightnings. I saw bolts dancing beneath the cloud over the notches in the palisades. The smell of

> "Gravestones tell truth scarcely fourty years.
> Generations pass while some trees stand, and old
> Families last not three Oaks."
> — Browne, *Urn Burial*, 1658

ozone came to us wetly.

"Soon the Buzzard Cult people will start dancing to call down the thunder," Took said.

"Why would they do that?"

"They revel in death even more than we do," he said. "They invite it. It's their way."

"I don't think this storm will need any help," I said. The sound of the thunder was like a kettledrum being beaten just in front of us.

I looked out past the wall and the burial mounds, the dried fields. The woods, lit by the coming storm, began to rock and bend. Wind and water smacked me in the face.

Lightning bolts sizzled beneath the cloud, walked across the sky, boiled inside the thunderhead. Thunder smashed at us.

There were torches in front of the temple mound, and chanting I couldn't quite catch through the wind and the noise.

"Let's go to the big mound," said Took.

People ran by, heading for the plaza. We ambled down that way, going instead to the big mound that had once been used for burials on the east side of the courtyard. We sat down.

The wind was whipping the straining woods. The thunder was as loud as a 155 going off next to your ears. The cloud leaned over us. A ragged wall cloud spun around, its top nearly touching the trees. The undersides of the clouds were green and purple.

"We're going to get hail," I observed, needlessly.

Took had one of his unfinished pipes out. He could have worked on it by the continuous lightning. I couldn't keep my eyes off the storm.

Over on the plaza Sun Man was atop the temple steps. Thatch from the hut roofs blew across like long snow. Torches went out.

The cold wet air hit us like fists. The hail hitting the River and the trees beyond sounded like an animal gnawing on them.

Lightning struck the palisade to the east. Thunder sounded like hot grease thrown on ice. Fist-sized hail started bouncing around like batting practice at the Astrodome. We got off the mound just as rain crashed into the village.

We made it to a hut belonging to Took's cousin, along with a few other relatives. The wind shrieked, rocking the mud-wattled walls. We stood in the doorway, looking out. The plaza was a deserted blur. There were a few torches under the eaves of the temple showing where everyone ran.

Lightning hit a hut across the village, setting the roof on fire in a screaming explosion. Hailstones strobed in the flashing light, like a sky filled with Christmas tree ornaments. The white sky went away and fires sprang up. People pulled others from the burning hut. One of them was hit with a hailstone, then the hail quit and the rain came in flat level sheets.

Thunder crashed. I thought my sphincter would open. Part of the hut we were in blew away. Rain came in lumps. We ran around inside bumping into each other and getting things up off the wet mud floor.

Then two things happened at once:

I saw the midwife and Sunflower coming between the huts, toward the plaza, carrying something.

And lightning hit the temple, exploding it.

People screamed and ran toward the temple mound, Took with them. I ran toward Sunflower.

The lightning was horrible. We could all be hit anytime. The wind and rain mauled us. I was soaked in a few steps. If the hail hadn't already stopped, I would be dead.

Flames lit up the night between the lightning bolts. The whole top of the mound was afire. Men were climbing up the temple walls, across the roof, cutting lashings, throwing handfuls of mud and dirt.

I reached Sunflower and the midwife. Sunflower looked up at me, the rain washing her face in streams. She and the midwife held a covered bundle between them. They said nothing. They didn't have to.

Between thunderclaps I could hear Sunflower crying softly.

More lightning hit the village, a real explosion of flying

sticks scattering in the air toward the north wall.

Now the Buzzard Cult people were dancing in the middle of the plaza, standing in one place, rocking back and forth on their feet, chanting some tune to themselves, not helping with fighting the fire or pulling people out of their huts.

Rain pressed us down. The whole roof of a hut gave way and sailed like a tumbleweed through the plaza, missing everyone. Wails and moans were starting all over the village, with real names, not ritual ones. People were getting hurt, crushed, burned, maybe killed.

I reached out and took the limp bundle from the midwife. I pulled Sunflower to me by the shoulder. She was weak, shaking. I guided her toward the temple mound.

Up on the mound they had some of the fire out, and most of the stuff was outside. People were still running around, Sun Man directing them to other parts of the village to fight other fires. He yelled to the women to get baskets and jugs and being them back. Everyone was outside the huts now, oblivious to the rain and the lightning.

Then we heard the rumbling like a freight train coming through the forest to the south, the sound of tearing trees rising above it.

Through the lightning I could see a low wall cloud.

Then the rain *stopped*, like a faucet turned off.

The roaring grew louder. Lightning flashed deep within the cloud, and we all saw the tornado hanging like a fat anaconda from the ragged clouds, heading straight for the fields and the village.

Through the roaring of the tornado I heard other things. In the stillness of everything else I heard a cricket chirp, and rain dripping from a roof. I heard someone's feet run through a small puddle. I heard the crackle of fire from the temple roof. I heard someone across the village say the word "basket."

Then the roaring became louder, like a volume knob being slowly turned up.

I started Sunflower up the temple steps.

"I can't go up there," she said.

"Yes you can," I said, and pulled her. She came with me. Everyone was transfixed watching the tornado tear up the trees. There were lightning flashes, but the thunder was drowned by the echoing roar.

The twister looked like a sideways S. Lumps that were trees, alligators, fish, boulders flashed and disappeared around its outside. The bottom was a haze of airborne garbage. Trees leaned in toward it from all directions, tearing away in the drowning roar and being sucked into the funnel. My ears popped.

Someone saw us.

"No," they said, "No!"

We had reached the top step. Sunflower, me, the dead child. I turned facing the tornado and held the bundle up over my head.

The screaming tornado reached the edge of the fields, ripped up leaves and dead vines, heading for the south wall.

I held the baby up as high as I could. Nobody tried to stop me. The lightning was a purple dance around the tornado funnel. The landscape looked like it would through the bottom of a Vick's Salve bottle.

The tornado lifted up.

It left the ground, broke contact with the dirt and debris, just outside the south wall. I felt my hair stand up. It was dark for a few seconds. The lightning quit for the first time in two hours.

Then a huge flat sheet of light enveloped everything. Up above my head, past Took and Sunflower's dead child, I saw it.

The tornado hung. I could see inside the funnel, straight up. I tingled from fear and static electricity, my hair glowing. The tornado roared above us, moved to the north majestically, as if a moving cliff hung over us, upside down. It roared louder, set down to the north of the fields, tearing up the woods again, moving toward the River.

Thunder fell. A gentle rain started, cool and slow. Lightning still played but the thunder got lower, farther off. The last of the flames went out on the broken-down temple.

Took came to us, put his arms around Sunflower. I lowered the baby, went back down the steps. The only man-made sound in the village was that of the Buzzard Cult dancers, who had stopped only at the first appearance of the tornado.

The midwife was gone when we reached the plaza. Some of Took's relatives joined us at the bottom of the steps.

From up above on the mound, Sun Man started a chant of thanksgiving, which everybody except Took and Sunflower and I joined in.

Before we reached our hut, stars were peeping out to the west.

The test trench, begun fifteen feet out, hit the large mound six feet off center to the left. William, Washington, and the diggers from Jameson's team took the trench only to the original ground level before Kincaid sent them in toward the mound itself.

"Do a one-foot profile, then on down," said Kincaid. "Bessie, make sure the grids stay marked. I don't want to lose anything on this one."

Jameson was fidgeting on the edge of the cut. He and Kincaid sent two of the diggers off to help unload the trucks, and helped with the digging to work off some of their nervous energy.

There were gathering clouds on the northern horizon. The day was becoming still and hot with a high hazy overcast. There was as yet no thunder and lightning to be seen even in the darker clouds.

Bessie kept running checks on the digging, drawing new profiles in her notebook, a cross section of the mound at one-foot intervals, ready to be filled in as they worked. She sketched quickly and surely, and had sixteen of them, numbered and in sequence, before the diggers had reached the center of the mound on their first one-foot cut.

Kincaid and Jameson waited until the workers had gone down off the mound's crest to the ground level on the other side. Then they lay on their sides, one to left and one to right, crawling the entire length of the cut from one end to the other, starting at opposite sides. They looked like they were playing a child's game, or were two thirsty men crawling across the desert in a newspaper cartoon.

The workers leaned on their shovels, talked, sweated and joked. Somebody said something really rich and they broke into hoots of laughter. Bessie jerked her head around at the sound.

B E S S I E

4

Kincaid and Jameson were oblivious. They finished their crawl, careful of the grid markers, and came to their feet, brushing dirt from their hands and clothing.

They had a hurried consultation, then went to the workers. The diggers went back around to the side they had begun the trench on. Once again they started a slow careful cut, a yard wide, another foot deep, from the edge of the mound, over the top, to the far side, carrying the dirt carefully over to the sifting screens as they worked, where others went through it.

Bessie knew it had probably taken the Coles Creek people who built these mounds at least a month to get them to this size, perhaps longer. They had carried basketfuls, skinfuls of dirt at a time, to raise it. The dirt had been dug with hoes made of the shoulder-blades of animals strapped to handles, or with shells, even scooped up by hand. Making a mound took a long time; they stood for hundreds, even thousands of years. They could be taken apart in a few days by skilled workers, or as had happened in a few disastrous cases, in a few minutes by treasure seekers with the use of grader blades and dynamite.

William and Washington could dig a trench straight as a ruler, never varying the depth by more than an inch or two, pretty quickly. Kincaid said William had azimuths for eyes. There were a couple more, including a white man named Griggs, on Jameson's team, who were good, and all could do fine work under William's directions.

The second one-foot cut went faster than the first, since they had already gone through the roots of the ground cover in the first foot. The diggers stopped, and once more Kincaid and Jameson made their long crawls, this time more slowly, and from the ends opposite to where they had started the time before. They met near the top of the mound.

"How you doing?" asked Kincaid.

They both laughed for a few minutes, then continued on. One of the guys from up on the bluff lugged a new watercan down, passing the dipper around among the workers who lay resting in the heat.

Kincaid finished, got up, took a dipperful of water and drank it down.

Jameson came around the mound, pulled a collapsible metal cup from his shirt pocket, opened it, dipped it in the watercan and took a sip.

"Bessie, come down here," said Kincaid.

The three put their heads together.

"There's no sign of an intrusion, on either of the sides. Either that, or the whole top has been taken off, which I doubt. We're going to assume, from now on, and until we find differently, that the mound is original."

"And it's possible," said Jameson, "that this may have been a religious platform, and has nothing in it. And that we'd be wasting our time on these one-foot profiles."

"Then what's next?" asked Bessie.

"Right straight through?" asked Kincaid.

Jameson nodded. They gave the instructions to William.

The camp shifted gears again, becoming not faster, but slower, smoother, as though it had more traction. Bessie could feel it. People moved more slowly but wasted no time. Things were put in order for the long haul, watercans appeared, a wheelbarrow line started, up to the sifting screens, where miniature mounds were starting.

Bessie sketched the left profile of the two-foot cut. There were the usual rounded forms where baskets of earth had been dumped and tamped, but Jameson and Kincaid were right — no intrusions. Only the differences in individual earthloads showed, and that one kind had been used for the lower and another for the upper, conical mound. Either the smaller mound had been built at a different, later time than the platform, or they had been built specifically of two kinds of earth — not unknown, but rare.

Everything about these mounds is uncommon, she thought. The location — below the bluff rather than on it — the shape, two connected mounds, and the strange platform and cone shape of the larger one — and their composition: aside from the horse bones, and the fact that *only* horse bones were in the smaller mound, there were also the two kinds of earth making up the larger one.

The laborers were in the test trench now. They were careful, but their shovels bit deep, carving into the mystery, throwing the layers of the past out into the waiting wheelbarrows.

Thunder rumbled.

A wind of relief blew across the digs, making the tents on the bluff crackle and flap.

the box

4

Smith's Diary   Oct 15

    I came out of my tent to go on Officer of the Guard duty just after sundown.

    The bluff was already dark behind us. Somebody had been fishing and was coming back with some catfish from the bayou.

    We had all turned into pretty decent fishermen in the last two weeks. The smell of cooking meat came from the cook shack. Tomorrow's breakfast and lunch. We weren't tired of venison yet.

    The loudspeaker was on. A lull was settling over the camp. People were sitting around talking. The sentries were in their bunkers toward the bayou and up on the bluff. There was a light on in Spaulding's tent, the only light not made by fires. There was laughter and low talk from the soldiers. I went up on the bluff and said hello to the guards.

    The moon was coming up like a pumpkin over the water. The camp was settling toward a night of sleep. The bayou turned into a flat tree-lined sheet of glass with an orange strip of moonlight in it. Bats flew across the face of the moon.

    Moonlight Serenade *came on the loudspeaker.*

    It was real neat.

It had snowed during the night. It was cold when I'd gone to sleep under my deerskin the night before. I woke sometime during the early morning with the tick-tick of ice pellets on the sides of the mud and wattle hut.

Outside, the village lay under ten centimeters of white. Took-His-Time stood in the doorway. Sunflower had stirred up the fire and sweet pinewood smoke filled the house.

"Winter's here," said Took.

L
E
A
K
E

5

"I didn't think it would snow here," I said.

"Usually doesn't."

We sat down to eat jerky and hominy but never got that far. There was a yell outside the doorflap.

"What now?" asked Sunflower.

"Come!" said Took-His-Time.

Hamboon Bokulla, the Dreaming Killer, stepped inside, followed by Moe. They began talking with Took so fast that I only caught every fifth word. Sunflower listened a minute, then picked up two pemmican bags and put jerky in them.

Moe and Dreaming Killer went outside. Took said something to Sunflower. She handed him the pemmican bags.

"Yaz," he said to me while rummaging in the pipestone pile, "there's something I have to do, and something you need to see."

"Sounds good, Took," I said. I didn't like Dreaming Killer at all and didn't think he was bringing any good news.

Took and Sunflower hugged each other as Took dropped something into the pipe bag. Then Sunflower turned and put her hand on my shoulder for a moment.

For some reason I was blushing as we left the hut. The

"In the beginning the whole world was like America."
— John Locke

four of us started off at a trot. Looking at snow is one thing. Running through it in moccasins is another.

———————

I was winded before we'd gone three kilometers. Took hadn't said anything since we left the hut. He had nothing but his knife and pipe bag with him. I had my bayonet and the short spear and club. Moe and Dreaming Killer looked like they were ready for a short war.

We headed northwest, away from the river. The snow squeaked and crunched under our feet. Moe, in the lead, was following some path I couldn't see. I just put my feet in Took's footprints, one after the other. I pulled my blanket tighter around my shoulders.

The land around us was totally different under the snow cover. Like something out of a Breughel painting — the sky was a green-gray, the far distance lost in a green smudge of darkness. Pools were slicks of green-gray ice. Snow hung on the tree limbs. Occasional flakes hit me between the eyes.

Another kilometer on we slowed, coming to one of the five-family hamlets surrounded by fields that were worked only in the summer. Ten or twenty people stood around surveying the devastation.

Two of the summer huts had been flattened. The place looked like a bulldozer had been through it. The snow and the ground under it had been plowed and churned. A compost heap was scattered, giving ripe steaming odors into the cold air. One of the deep seed-corn burial pits had been torn up. Half the seed was gone, the rest scattered over the village yard. A set of gigantic smudged tracks led into the village from the north and out of the devastation to the west.

Moe and Dreaming Killer talked with the villagers quietly, then we started off after the big footprints.

"About six bowshots more," Took said under his breath. "Be very quiet."

I was as quiet as I could be, rasping my lungs out in the cold air. The snow was falling a little harder, the sky turning a milky white.

A man stood in the pathway ahead, pointing to a slight rise, moving his spear slowly to warn us.

We slowed to a walk, then Moe began a crouching shuffle, and waved Took up the rise beside him. We spread out, Took dropped to the ground, and we crawled the last few meters to the small rise. I started to look up over it, but Moe put a warning hand on my arm.

There was the sound of breaking and shuffling close by. To me it sounded like a car sliding off an icy road into a ditch.

Took reached in his bag, pulled out some shaped thing, slowly came to his knees, then stood.

"Oh, old one!" he said quietly and slowly, so even I could follow each word, "I have your spirit, I have your strength in this rock." He held up the pipestone. "Go your way in peace this time. We will not harm you. But do not come again to our fields, or we will have you."

Then he held the pipestone up again and opened his hands toward the far side of the rise. He put the stone back in his bag.

Moe and Dreaming Killer stood up then. So did I.

I shouldn't have. I almost sat back down again.

Imagine a mountain that has wandered away from its range. A mountain made of brown hair, immense against the sky and the pond. Its hair was red-brown and black, shaggy, and hung all the way down to the ground.

Its head was four meters from the earth. From its front two long crisscrossing white tusks pointed out and up. Humps of fat rode on its head and the tops of its shoulders. The long snakelike trunk moved from the racked ice of the pond to its mouth and back again in a slow graceful curve.

The mouth and ears were hidden in the hair. Only the eyes, black like two pools of tar, showed clearly through.

It dwarfed everything. The frozen pool and the landscape looked too small to contain it. Nothing that big was alive.

We stood for a moment before it noticed us. It turned to face us, its tree-trunk legs crunching ice, and stood stock still. So did we.

It was forty meters away. It raised its trunk and blew out a clot of water in a snorting spray, then made a noise I'll never forget, half tuba, half diesel, which turned into a bass note that hung on the wind.

I felt some of the frozen mist from its trunk on my face. I really wanted to run then but couldn't, any more than you can run in a dream.

It looked at us with those tar-drop eyes, then turned slowly, oh so slowly, and moved across the shallow end of the pond toward a dark tangle of woods to the west.

It stopped once, behemoth, leviathan, monster, and raised its trunk and called again, tusks out. It had a red fringe of beard around its mouth, streaked with black and gray. The tusks hung straight out while it trumpeted, three meters from the ground.

Its call echoed through the woods and the white countryside. There was a crashing of tree limbs and thump of heavy footfalls and it was gone.

The only sign that it had been there was the broken surface of the pond where chunks of ice washed slowly back and forth.

It called again, far away, then we heard no more.

Snow began to hit us in the face, a few flakes at first, then more. The wind picked up. We turned and walked back toward home.

My heart was as loud as a drum. I wondered why the others couldn't hear it.

"Not many of those left," said Dreaming Killer.

"Damn good thing," said Moe.

The director showed up a few hours later with the office staff. They came in four trucks and two sedans. The top of the bluff was beginning to look like a Ford dealership.

The storm threatened. The trench had reached four feet deep on the northwest side of the big mound. Kincaid was poking around in the test cut.

The director was a small man named Dr. Perch. He was nattily dressed in a suit and a floppy-brimmed hat. He wore thick glasses. He had been chairman of the anthropology department since there had been one. (There was a joke that he had held the measuring tape for Squier and Davis when they were researching their *Ancient Monuments of the Mississippi Valley*, which had come out in 1848. That wasn't true, but he had helped Cyrus Thomas with the *Report on the Mound Explorations of the Bureau of Ethnology*, which took up 730 pages of the Twelfth Annual Report of 1890-91. And he had not been in the field since then.)

Bessie led Dr. Perch to the sorting tent. She showed him the equine skulls, the cartridges, the potsherds and the mound profiles. Perch studied them without saying a word.

Wind whipped through the campsite, the tents shaking like sails on a ship. Across the bayou the storm gathered, like nightfall in reverse.

Dr. Perch said, "Looks like a real blow coming. We'll go back to the hotel. Make sure everything's battened down so we can start photographing tomorrow. I'm going to get on the phone to the governor's office, although he's on some damn speech-making tour over in Mississippi somewhere. You'd think he'd have more sense than to leave the state after they tried to impeach him five times this spring. He must have all the legislators locked up in the parish jail."

"What are you going to do?" asked Bessie.

"Keep those damn floodgates closed above and open below, if I can. That's a start."

"People are going to be upset if this thing goes wrong," she said.

Perch looked at her over his thick glasses. "If this thing does go wrong, and we both know what we mean by that, you, Kincaid, and I are all looking for jobs. I don't believe this stuff" — he pointed around the sorting tent — "for one minute. But if you and Kincaid and Jameson are putting your jobs on the line, so am I. And I'm too old to look for honest work."

Perch and his staff took two of the cars and one truck with them back town.

Kincaid called from the mound.

"Bessie, come get me the minute Perch gets here."

"He's already gone," she yelled to him, then walked down the bluff.

━━━━━━━━

Kincaid tried to light his pipe with one of the big kitchen matches he always carried. Grit flew into Bessie's eyes; the wind picked up again.

"What did he think?" asked Kincaid, giving up on the pipe.

"He's calling the governor about the floodgates."

Kincaid laughed. "I can see the governor letting farmers drown because of what Perch says. I doubt the governor knew there were Indians in this state once."

"Where's Jameson?" asked Bessie.

"Under the tarp on Mound 2B. He wanted another look before the rain. Who's that?"

Bessie looked around where Kincaid stared. Up on the bluff, amid all the activity, one person stood still. Bessie didn't recognize him as from the staff. He was gazing down at the mounds. He wore a tall-crowned western hat, a dark vest and khaki shirt. His pants were patched. He held a knapsack under one arm.

"The curious are here already," said Kincaid. "May be one of LaTouche's. Better go find out. I'll take another quick run through the trench before we get the tarps down." He sighted toward the storm. A lightning bolt silhouetted the woods on the other side of the water.

Bessie hurried up toward the tents. She met Washington on the way down.

"Know who that is?" she asked, pointing at the stranger.

"No, ma'am, but William was talkin' to him a few minutes ago."

William was coming out of the sorting tent.

"Oh, him? He said his name was Bob Basket. He looks just like an Indian to me, Miss Bessie. He said he heard we were tearing up them mounds and wanted to take one last look at them. I told him he could stand right on the edge of the bluff there, but don't get in anybody's way, and don't go down to the mounds. He's been standing there for an hour or so."

There was a frying noise from across the bayou. A gray slab of rain stretched both ways as far as the eye could see. The woods disappeared, and the faraway tin roof of the Crimstead house faded from sight. Then the waters of the Suckatoncha buckled and seethed with rain on the far side.

"Get everything covered up," yelled Bessie to the crews on the bluff.

She ran to check the windows on the office staff trucks. She put one windshield up and snapped the canvas cover in place. A few raindrops the size of fists beat the ground around her, sending up little crowns of dust.

Thunder screamed close by.

The wind and rain hit her in level sheets.

Bessie dove for the nearest tent.

the box

5

Smith's Diary   Oct 17

They call us the Music People.

I never thought about it. In any kind of primitive society, you don't have music unless you have people making it right then and there. Without music, there's nothing but natural noises; people talking, birdsongs, squawks, all that.

That must have been the first thing they noticed about us.

What we noticed about them first is that they don't look like movie Indians.

They're tattooed, a lot of the ones we've seen. They have feathers, but not many braids. A lot of them have shaved heads, the men, that is; the few women we've seen have their hair up in a sort of bun or French twist on the top or sides of their heads, keeping it out of the way.

Their tattoos are weird — circles, lightning bolts, strange designs with hands and tears, skulls, birds, snakes, a sort of three-sided swastika, like a bent Y.

Their skins range from a dark brown to a very light copper color. Some of them wear these big ear spools, like those lip things you always used to see Ubangis wear in cartoons, only these stretch their earlobes all out of shape.

A couple of them have pointy heads, though they seem to be intelligent, not microencephalic at all. From rumor I hear they are from much farther north, people who have married into the tribe we're dealing with.

Splevins gave us all a briefing on what we know so far. These people represent one or two villages which belong to a sort of loose-knit bigger tribe, on both sides of the Mississippi. They are pretty advanced in the arts (I've seen some of their handiwork; it's beautiful in a strange kind of way) and minor sciences (they work metal cold, they have flood-irrigation agriculture, mainly corn, beans, and squash) and are at peace with everyone for fifty kilometers in all directions.

From best guesses, they speak a sort of proto-Muskeogan language among themselves, and have a well-developed sign language with which to communicate with others (and us). They worship various totem animals (this tribe is part of the larger Turtle clan) and they have a matriarchically descended chief system. (They call their chiefs Sun Men, because they worship the sun; these Sun Men are both spiritual and active leaders of the villages. Their most important Sun Man, who lives some thirty kilometers away, they call the Sun King, which conjures up visions of Louis XIV*th* with tattoos and feathers.) They have great reverence for their dead, whom they place in mounds of earth, raised around the cremated (in the case of nobles) or buried remains of the dead.

(There seems to be another religious movement within the larger one having to do with the actual worship of death itself — hence all the tattoos with the tears, hands, eyes and snakes. We learned that about half of each of the villages belongs to this death cult.)

Some of their mounds are twenty meters high, great ceremonial places with temples atop them, for the big sun worships each year. Mostly the mounds are within their villages or just outside them. The ones outside they bury their dead in; those inside are for the temples.

Splevins and Putnam have actually seen the Indians' village — they went yesterday. Then they came back and gave us the briefing.

They are an industrious clean people, who should be able to help us in many ways, and we them.

The bad news is that we are the only black or white people they have ever seen. No Nordics, no one who could be thought of as Spanish or French, no Irish, no Chinese. The only other peoples they know about (aside from their large confederation) are some hunting tribes who live far to the northwest, who they trade with once a year in the summer, and a couple of emissaries (who sound a lot like Mexican Amerindians to Splevins) who drop by every three years or so to tell *them what a good thing they have going way down south.*

They have never seen horses before.

They have never seen iron or steel, though they do work with copper and gold.

Splevins is of the inescapable conclusion that we are in some time before the European discovery of America.

(It would take a CIA man that long to realize it.)

We have missed the mark by 400 years, maybe more. We are stuck in this past, unless they figure out something Up There in 2002.

Well, now we have a 400 year head start on the future, rather than only seventy. Time for SDO duty.

PS: The Indians seem to like In the Mood *best when they visit.*

Sun Man woke up the world like he always did.

"Yee-Yeee-Yee!" he yelled from his housemound, just as the edge of the sun peeked over the woods from the far side of the River.

I had been awake a few minutes; something in my body always woke me up before the old man screamed bloody murder every day. Took-His-Time and Sunflower stirred in their skins. It was late winter, almost spring. The trees were beginning to bud, though this far south they'd only lost the last of their leaves two months before.

The sap was rising in everything, including me.

"Has he ever missed a morning?" I asked Sunflower as she got up. Her figure was back after the pregnancy that had ended the night of the tornado.

"Not yet," she said. She went out to perform her matutinal ablutions.

"Once," said Took from his skins, "we thought he was Going to Meet the Woodpecker. He had them prop him up in a doorway. He didn't make much of a noise when he yelled, but he did wake up the people next to the plaza. Then he got well again. That was ten years ago."

"What happens if Sun Man doesn't yell?"

"The sun doesn't come up," said Took. "Is all your stuff ready?"

Two weeks before, Took had been rummaging in his pile, then looked at me and said, "Time to go to the Hill."

"Shit Hill?" I asked. Took didn't usually make a big deal of things like that.

"No. Pipe Hill. Five days up the River. If you're going to

L E A K E 6

"To keep our eyes open longer were but to act our Antipodes. The huntsmen are up in America, and they are already past their first sleep in Persia."
— Browne, *The Garden of Cyrus*, 1658

be a pipemaker you'll have to learn sometime. See some country, lug some big rocks around, break your fingers, stuff like that."

"Well, things have been pretty dull since the Old One came around. When do we go?"

"Winter's usually dull," said Took-His-Time. "Spring's coming; lots to do then. Flower Wars. The traders come back. Planting. The Black Drink Ceremony, the Wood-pecker Dance, then harvest. The year'll fairly fly. This will be the last chance to get new pipestone for seven, eight months. I'm running out of effigy stuff."

"Like you used for the Old One's spirit?"

"Just the stuff. Hell, there can't be more than four or five of those things left. But sometimes we get bears, sometimes buffalo come so thick and we kill so many you yarp when you smell bison meat, that I have to drive them away. The paroquets and the pigeons. There's nothing better than a couple of dozen paroquets for supper, but after a week or so they've eaten your fields up. So I have to make a paroquet pipe so they'll leave."

"Can't you just use what you've got here?" One whole corner of the hut was filled with fist-sized stones.

"Uh, no," he said. "For pipes, I could use sumac root if I wanted to, burn a guy's lips right off. But for the effigy stuff, I need certain kinds of stone. Don't ask. Trade secret. I'll have to show you when we get there."

That was two weeks ago. This morning we were leaving, which is why Took asked about my gear.

I started to ask him about getting the rocks back down the River, when Sunflower came back in. She kicked us on the bottoms of our feet.

"Up, lazybones," she said as she kicked. "Guys are already fishing."

Out of habit I packed the radio beacon in my gear. Not that we wouldn't be out of range a day up the River, but because I thought I should. I put the carbine and some ammo in with my things, but kept the carbine wrapped in its greased skins.

While we got ready, I watched a neighbor lady scraping a fox skin. Sunflower was in and out of the hut. An old man, much older even than Sun Man, really ancient, sat in front of his hut and smoked.

Smoking accounted for about fifty percent of a guy's time. Took had a thriving business which I was slowly learning. He made all the pipes for individuals, for the religious ceremonies, for nabob Sun Men in far villages across the River. Every guy in the village had his own private tobacco patch that he cultivated. You didn't touch another person's patch. Each patch had a secret combination of herbs, tobacco, and weeds that the owner grew and smoked. Some of them smelled like burning tire factories to me.

Took-His-Time, being the guy who made all the pipes for everybody, was not allowed to smoke. It was part of the religion.

We carried our gear through the village, out the gate and down to the River, where the canoe we had fixed up the day before waited. Several people waved good-bye to us.

———

"Paddling up this River," I said, "is like rowing through molasses."

Took looked at me from the bow, his eyebrow raised.

"Uh, honey," I said, finding the nearest Greek word. He and I still did most of our talking in Greek, although I had picked up enough of the mound-builder talk to sound at least like a simpleton when I talked. I could say things like "I own spear. Spear very straight." I could understand a lot more than I could say, except when people got excited (which happened fairly often) and talked fast. Pretty good for three months, I thought.

"It's a lot better coming back down," said Took. "Then it's like paddling through olive oil."

———

When we camped out the first night, it was like we were the only two people on the continent. We were on a little raised place back from the water. In the summer here the mosquitoes would only have been the size of moths, not the size of sparrows like they would be down at the River itself.

We had a fire going. Though it was late winter, there were still plenty of night noises. Alligators grunted, frogs chugged, birds screamed, bats flew over. There were snuffles and snorts all around.

Overhead the stars were like frost. Orion, the mighty hunter, bent his bow across the sky. On Cyprus during the blackouts, even after the Big War back Up There, the nights had never been this dark, the stars never so many or so bright.

Took's face was outlined in the starlight.

"What do you call that?" I asked, pointing at what I thought was Mars.

"I don't call it anything much," he said. "The Traders call it Ares. The Northerners call it Loke. When we call it anything, we call it the One That Moves Backward Every Two Years."

"Ever wonder why it does that?" I asked.

"Because the Woodpecker told it to," said Took.

"When you were with the Traders as a boy, did the Traders talk about the stars?"

"All the time. They were great sailors, used them to navigate and tell time and things. Even so, I had to tell them they were way off."

"How?"

"Well, I used to count the days I was with them, and when I got into the seven hundreds, I knew it had been more than two years. One time they were talking about calendars and dates and stuff; they said something that was wrong and I told them.

"'What do you mean?' they asked me.

"'There's been half a day extra since you swiped me,' I said.

"'What do you mean, half a day?' they asked.

"'Well, every four years there's an extra day.' I said.

"'We've been using this here calendar for five hundred years now,' they said.

"'Then you're probably planting your crops in late fall,' I said.

"'You're twelve years old and a heathen, what do you know?' they said.

"I told them to look up in the sky at the One That Moves Backward Every Two Years, and decide who knows more. I wasn't as good at it as Sun Man's granduncle used to be, but I told them we had this big carved rock two days' journey downriver from the village I was born in that told us when the extra days were coming. Somebody had copied it from the Huastecas a long time ago. All our people go down there and figure out when to do things by it. They didn't believe it, of course.

"That was fifteen years ago, before they really started trading with the Huastecas. Since then they've had this big conference with their priests, and all the East has thrown away its old calendars and got new ones.

"They no longer plant in the winter, I'm told." Took leaned back on his skins and went to sleep.

I watched the pale dot of Mars, like a red nailhead driven into the sky.

———

The second and third days out, the villages got fewer and farther apart on the west bank of the River, while they got thicker on the east.

On the west the land lay flat with fewer trees. We passed a herd of buffalo, thousands and thousands, stretching as far as the eye could see, on the third morning upriver.

"They're gonna eat good this spring," said Took, pointing toward the next village on the west side of the River. "The buffalo must have come in late yesterday, otherwise hunters would have been at them by now."

The villagers way across the River to the east were already putting out canoes. They'd seen the buffaloes. Their village was two or three times as large as Took's, with dozens of mounds, some of them fifteen meters tall.

"They build 'em right, don't they?" I said, pointing.

"Way upriver," said Took, "they got a place Kohoka,

bigger than all the villages put together. There's a mound there five times taller, twenty times as long as that one. They've been working on it a thousand years, though, and there must be fifty thousand of them at it. They should have run out of dirt by now."

I whistled.

"Hell, Yaz," said Took. "Give us fifty thousand people, we'd build a mound so big you'd have to put a trench in it for the moon to roll through."

On the fourth night we turned up a small tributary and made camp about four kilometers up it. There were already a couple of canoes put in up and down the bank, but the fires were already out and the people were asleep.

"Go to sleep, Yaz," said Took, bedding down in the bottom of the canoe. "We'll need it tomorrow."

When we woke up the next morning, Took put me to work building a raft.

"Why make the raft first?" I asked. "We don't have anything to put on it yet."

"We make the raft first," said Took, "because when we get back here with the cargo, we'll be too tired to build a raft. Trust me."

While I dragged dead wood down and lashed it together, Took was shaping long wedges out of hardwood sapling and working them in a fire he'd made. We made good progress. By noon, Took waved me to follow him. He picked up his wedges, a maul, and rawhide ropes.

We went through a small woods, following a hard-packed trail, then came out to a clearing. Above it was a small hill, and on the hill two or three guys were hammering away at the rocks.

We climbed through small rocks and scree. They hurt my feet, even through my boots. How Took did it in his moccasins, I don't know.

"Hell, Took-His-Time!" yelled one of the men who was flailing away at a rock five times his size.

"Hey, Tree-Gum!" said Took, going up to him. "Meet my friend Yazoo." We held wrists a second.

He was a wiry old man, and he was farting so much I thought he had frogs in his breechcloth.

"Breaking the kid in?" asked Tree-Gum.

"Sort of." Took looked at the sweating old man. "Aren't you too old to be doing this by yourself?"

"Oh, I'm not taking a load, I'm getting a heart-stone."

Took looked at the three-ton boulder. "Well, we'll be here all day. Come over to our fire tonight."

"Thanks," said Tree-Gum, then went back to jumping up and down on a sapling he'd wedged into the rock.

We went farther up.

Took leaned close. "He's getting the exact center out of the boulder. Big medicine of some kind, something he can only do himself. You don't ask about stuff like that. He's from two days upriver from here. He must be eighty years old."

Took was running his hand across a rock face with a fracture in it. "Here," he said, taking my hand, putting it up to the stone. "Feel that?"

There was a discontinuity in the texture as well as color across the break. Above, it felt like dry sandstone; below the crack the rock felt wet and greasy, smooth to the touch.

"It feels like a salamander," I said.

"Just the stuff we want," he said.

"How much of it?"

"The whole damn thing," said Took.

"Jesus."

―――――――――――

By pitch dark we had holes punched in, wedges driven, and levers ready on a section two meters by one and a half.

"Tomorrow morning," said Took.

I followed him as well as I could through the blackness. We made it back to camp. Took stirred up the ashes and got the fire going. We ate some jerky, pemmican, and dried nuts.

Tree-Gum came over, bringing something in a leather bottle that smelled like root beer. "Here," he said. "Have some." We did.

He warmed his hands at the fire. "Damned winters are getting colder," he said. Took told him about the visit of the mammoth.

"Hell, I ain't ever seen one of those," said Tree-Gum. "Don't much want to, either. You know the Huastecas were all the way up here last year? They been sending envoys farther up every year, north along the River. Getting ready for trade, I guess. They've whupped up on everybody down there they can, I reckon. Now nothin's left but to buy and sell."

He let another huge fart, and fanned the air with his hands. Then he stared into the fire. "We got to find a new Hill, Took-His-Time. Talked with a couple dozen pipe-makers up and down the River. Pipe Hill here's gonna give out in twenty, thirty years. Never thought I'd see it. Gonna be up to you young 'uns, like you and your friend Yaz here, to find it. I'm sure too old to go traipsing around these hills.

"This has been a good Pipe Hill, though. Taken many a thousand pipes out of it, yes sir."

Then he was quiet. After a while he got up and stretched. "Well, give my regards to Sun Man and that no-good sister of his. Come up to the place sometime. I imagine you'll be gone a couple of days by the time I get through here."

We waved good-bye, and he walked out of the firelight.

———————————

"Look out below!" yelled Took, and the only guy working farther down the hill scrambled up even with us.

"Gardy-Loo!" I said.

"Heave-ho," said Took. We heave-hoed. There was a groan in the early morning stillness, then a snap as one of our sapling levers broke. We pounded another one in and pulled again. Cables stood out in Took's arms. I thought my temples were going to burst.

Then everything moved and I fell down. The hemisphere of pipestone separated itself from the rock face and began to crash and roll its way down the hill.

It took a propitious spin and went off through the woods toward the tributary, taking small trees with it.

The other pipemakers applauded.

"I'll be Woodpecker-damned," said Took. We grabbed up our ropes and headed off down the hill. As we got near the woods I looked back. Tree-Gum and the others were already back at their tasks. The old man was jumping up and down on a lever. Something slipped; a large crack he'd made in the boulder closed back up, splitting wedges. He shook his fist at it. For a second, you couldn't tell whether he was taking the rock apart or putting it back together again.

We found the rock less than fifty meters from the water.

"Lucky lucky lucky," said Took. "Here, grab this rope."

———————————

Lucky or not, the sun was going down by the time we were ready to go.

The rock was lashed in the center of the raft. We'd built a small platform of logs across the back and made a skin tent on it. Took had made a sweep from small trees.

We tied the canoe to the raft and put out into the current of the tributary. My muscles were all gone. It was a good thing the water pushed us along. I didn't have the strength to pole, sweep, or paddle.

Took stretched out in the tent. "Uh, what should I do?" I asked.

"Nothing. Turn right when we get to the River. You'd find turning left extremely hard. Call me before the light's all gone and we'll put in."

He was snoring almost immediately. I watched the horizon bisect the sun behind us. There was still plenty of light left. The trees thinned, then we were onto the delta. I never really knew when we got on the River — the tributary widened, then we turned south and the River itself was around us, the tributary gone.

A gar croaked ahead, and the frogs started up. The first bat of the evening dipped over the water, and then the sky turned honey-gold to the west, making the River an amber mirror. Herons waded in an indentation in the shoreline.

The River turned slowly ahead until it went out of sight, kilometers away. A whippoorwill cranked up, long and lonely somewhere toward the sunset.

"Huck and Jim," I said.

"What?" said Took.

"Nothing. We'd better put in."

Took leaned his head out of the tent.

"Some big-ass river, huh?"

the box

6

Smith's Diary   Oct 21

The word is that they are getting sick.

Spaulding has restricted everyone but the medics from contact with them. The doc is out at the second village with a team, trying to find out what's wrong.

At least two of the Indians have died. They developed colds, running bloody noses, fevers, and then they died.

We were so careful, too. Up There, we had every shot you could think of, besides the usual stuff. Our arms and butts were sore for days, we had low grade fevers, and felt like shit for a week we had so many shots. But that was a month ago. We should be immune to everything.

Which doesn't mean we weren't carriers.

The doc is back.

There are more of them sick and one more has died in the second village. Except for the sick ones, the village is deserted. They had buried one in the common mound, but the rest left before the other two died. It looked like they had been getting ready for another burial ceremony but they dropped everything and ran.

The team took smears and samples, and hope to find out something, with our limited resources. We certainly can't manufacture vaccines here, if that's what it takes.

Spaulding told the doc to go out only with an armed guard if they left the camp again. The doctor didn't think it was wise but didn't argue very long either.

I hope this all blows over. We have enough problems already. They gave me the job of thinking up a few scenarios. They can't do anything without an agenda.

They looked like a thousand parrots had committed suicide for them.

L E A K E 7

There were six of them, plus their servants, runners and so forth.

They reached the village about an hour after we first heard their horns and conch shells. They were shorter than Took's people, darker than the standard, and two of them had mustaches.

They were the Meshicas, the Huastecas. Took told me they came this time every year to meet with Sun Man and arrange a Flower War with all us hefty moundbuilder types.

They smiled a lot while they were here. They looked as if the smiles were pasted on.

Snappy dressers, too, if your idea of beauty is to throw peacocks, roosters and pheasants together in a blender.

I was glad to see them go. Everybody's breechcloth looked dingy and tell-tale gray while they were around.

"Antiquity — I like its ruins better
than its reconstructions."
— Joubert

The rain slammed against the tents. They began to leak around the pole grommets. The walls moaned like living things.

Bessie sat on a camp stool. Though there was a roaring wind outside, the tent was close and hot. When lightning blasted nearby, they could see through the walls, see the cook tent, part of the bluff, the nearby trees slanting in the storm.

A bolt hit something near the bayou. Bessie and the others jerked; she saw individual raindrops printed on her eyesight like a photograph, hanging still in their fall toward the earth, trapped by the lightning. Thunder screamed instantly.

"Lordy," said William, "what a storm!"

"I'm not so much worried about this bad storm, or one or two, if they'll quit," said Bessie. "If the rains keep on, the bayou will rise and they'll have to throw the gates above here. All this work will just go under."

Ned and Leroy were quiet, hands folded on their laps. Bessie could tell they were uncomfortable being in the tent with her. They were younger and newer to the job than the other workers, and were still uncomfortable around Kincaid and the others.

"I sure hope Dr. Kincaid got to cover," said William. "Last I saw he was just getting out of the trench while we was floppin' the tarps down."

Then Bob Basket spoke for the first time.

"Two years ago," he began. Bessie jerked her head around toward him. She had not seen him come in, in the rush for the tent. He was seated on the ground cloth toward the back, legs crossed. He still wore his hat. His long face looked like a gnarled limb in the dim light from the kerosene lamp by the bulging tentflap.

As Basket spoke, there was another gigantic flash and crack. Bessie saw him illuminated, white and searing, in

BESSIE

6

her gaze, outlined by a crooked lightning bolt that dug itself into the woods beyond the road. She saw beyond the tent walls the outline of the LaTouche house. She saw something else, too, in Basket.

"Two years ago," he said again as the thunder died, "the river left its banks and was forty miles wide, and killed many thousands of people. The government got excited and now wants to make the river flow like a creek.

"But in the time of my father's father's great-great-grandfather, it rained once for three years. There were never more than two days with sunshine. There were no crops. There was no summer and no winter either, just rain and fog, the woods, the fields, the sky lost in gray.

"The second year the ground could hold no more water. The rivers started to rise more and more. The little creeks spread out and joined each other like hands of water. All the grass had died in the rain and the waters covered that. All the weeds had died and the creeks covered them. The small trees were still standing, and the waters began to rise up their trunks.

"Our people began to be worried. Where will we go? What can we do? Already dead buffalo and deer and wolves were floating in the water, more and more. Snakes climbed into trees, and when the waters rose up them, they hung like vines and fell into the water and swam to larger trees. They waited there for the waters to rise into them.

"A catfish the size of a bear swam between the huts of our village and paused at the knees of the shaman, swimming around him in slow circles.

"He wants us to follow him, said the shaman. Into your canoes as fast as you can.

"So the people got into their canoes and went to the village center, and when they were ready, the catfish turned and swam past the chief's house, and over the fields, and our people followed, paddling their canoes. And the catfish swam slowly so that even the weakest of our people could keep up in their boats.

"As he swam, our people passed the mounds of the Old Ones who were here before us. The mounds were washing away into the rising waters, exposing their ornaments and weapons, their bones and grave goods. We watched many of them fall into the rushing streams, large mounds, small ones, ones without anything in them, some as full of things as a store in Baton Rouge.

"And then the catfish brought my people to this place where we are now. It brought them to the mound out there, and they pulled their canoes up on it, all ten thousand of them. They had all remembered the mounds to be very small ones, below the bluff, but they all stood on its top in comfort, and the bluff was nowhere to be seen in all the moving waters.

"The big fish turned and left, swimming away without looking back, but some said they saw it turn into a crow and fly away into the rain and darkness before it got out of sight.

"So my people stayed there for another year, and they planted their corn, and it grew, and they were content, and got used to the rain, the waters of which had covered everything in all directions, as far as their eyes could see.

"Then one day a year later it quit raining, and the sun came out and the waters began to drop away, so that first the trees on the bluff, then the top of the bluff, then the trees toward the bayou, then the saplings and the shrubs and grass all came into view as the sun dried everything out.

"And my people noticed now that the mounds were very small, and that the crops were only a few inches tall, and that their canoes were the size of toys. They noticed also that the bluff and the trees were much higher than the mound, and they wondered greatly about the whole matter.

"But the shaman had them give thanks to the catfish and the Old Ones who built the mounds, and the crow (if there was one) and to the miracle of the whole thing.

"And so they harvested their little crops and picked up their toy canoes and they walked back many miles to where their village was and started all over again.

"And they named this place the Great Big Small Place and they remembered it in their prayers until the white men made them quit praying to things they could see and hear.

"All this happened in my father's father's great-great-grandfather's time, and that is the way they told it to me. I see it has stopped raining."

Bessie looked around. It had stopped. There was the constant drip of water running off the tentflap, the sound of a small rivulet gurgling down the bluff. She didn't know how long she had listened to Basket talk, his face shining in the glow of the lightning and the lamp.

Ned and Washington were asleep. Leroy stared ahead of him.

Bessie climbed to her feet, took the lamp, opened the tentflap and stepped outside. Her feet squished in the mud. There was a cool wind blowing from the north, and lightning still flashed in the east.

The other tents were wet glows on the bluff line, light and shadows from the lamps inside them falling on the dripping boxes and the wheels of the trucks parked around them. Father back toward the road, there was a single lamp burning at the LaTouche place. Away to the west-northwest over the bayou, she could see the light from the boat landing in front of the Crimstead house.

Below her she saw the dim outlines of the mounds under their tarps and covers.

She saw too, in the darkness for the first time, that there was a slight depression, extensive in area, to the northwest of the mounds, where the ground sloped off toward the bayou. She had walked over it dozens of times on the way between Mound One and the connected mounds. She was sure it was marked on the contour maps.

She turned back inside the tent, looking past the sleeping black men.

"There *was* some kind of settlement here," she said.

She looked wildly around.

Bob Basket was gone, only a wet place on the ground cloth showing where he had sat.

the box

7

Smith's Diary   November 1

I went to see Kilroy.

I told him the brass told me to come up with a real long-term plan. Not like the seventy-year plan we'd started with, the one more than a hundred people had worked on.

"Great," he said, "just great. How long?"

"At least five hundred years," I said.

"I'm not going to be around that long, and neither will any of us."

"That's just the kind of plan they want, Specialist," I said. "How do we go about setting up anything that'll take half a millennium? What are we supposed to do, kidnap Indian kids, brainwash 'em, set up an operation that'll select Stevenson in '52 rather than Eisenhower? Or what?"

"If I'm supposed to figure all this out," said Kilroy, "why am I just a grunt? I thought only officers had that much foresight."

"It's not just for them," I said. "It's for me, too."

"It's you?" he asked. "You want me to come up with a five-hundred-year plan for you? While I pull bunker guard and shitburning detail? For your amusement, or what?"

"To see if there's any reason for keeping up this whole charade," I said.

He put down the bottle of Indian honey wine he'd been drinking from. "Oh," he said. "Free will versus determination? That kind of stuff?"

"It's not all of us, and everybody, anymore." I tried to make myself clear. "It's just every one of us, alone. By ourselves. If there's a plan, anything, it'll be easier for all of us. Don't you see?"

"Yes. First thing is, we'll have to make lots of babies. I'm ready!"

"That's pretty stupid, Kilroy," I said.

"Probably. But for an officer, ma'am, you've got great legs."

"Uh," I said.

"I'll get on it," he said. "God knows, I'll have to think about this."

I started to go. Then I said, "Thank you."

"That's what I'm here for," he said. And made a fake smile. Then he added, "You're the only one who really cares about any of this. Not just the mission but what happens to us."

"Shut up," I said. "Get some sleep." Then I left.

The canoes came across the River, row on row. They were full of guys dressed in their best feathers, their brightest jewelry, their gaudiest clothes.

They carried their best weapons, too. Spears, atl-atls, bows, axes, clubs, shields, reed and leather armor, and knives. They could have wrecked any bar in Hong Kong.

But we were going out to meet the Huastecas for a ritual battle, a flower-fight they called it, and the way it was explained to me, the idea was to capture as many of the other guys as you could, not to kill them.

"Don't worry," said Took, as we watched the dugouts slide up the shore and the warriors jump out, whooping and hollering. "When you see some of our people knock one of the Huastecas down, jump on him. Everybody will think you're a fine fellow."

"What's the purpose?" I asked.

Took looked at me. "Well, you can't have wars with your own people, can you?"

"What happens to the ones who are captured?"

"Ours, or theirs?"

"Uh, theirs."

"Oh, they ransom them, usually. Mostly for pretty stuff. Clothes, ornaments. The Huastecas make nice rings and things."

"What about ours?"

"Well, we usually try to ransom them, and they do send some of them back, but not all."

"What happens to the ones they don't send back?"

"I guess they eat them," said Took.

We fanned out, maybe two thousand of us in all, as agreed. I knew what Custer must have felt like on that bluff

> "The great mutations of the world are acted, our time may be too short for our designs."
> — Browne, *Urn Burial*

L
E
A
K
E

8

over the Little Big Horn, only now I was part of it. We were a day out of the village, heading west. We skirted the edge of some bayous. We headed through open rolling grasslands toward the setting sun.

At one bayou, Sun Man's people, Took, and I broke away from the rest of the main group. We walked through water up to our knees, under cypresses and Spanish moss (I've got to think of some other name for it) until we reached an opening in the waterway.

The trees here grow in a circle maybe two hundred meters across. All except for one. It was the biggest cypress I'd ever seen in my life, maybe eighty meters tall, five hundred or a thousand years old, maybe older. It was nothing but a trunk, except for one limb that started halfway up. The top of the tree was missing.

I noticed then that the Dreaming Killer and his Buzzard Cult people weren't with us. I asked Took.

"Religious differences," he said.

Sun Man raised his arms and yelled three times, like he does every morning. I caught enough of his chant to know that he was calling on the Big Woodpecker. Then we marched back out of the swamps and rejoined the holiday crowd heading for the battle site.

"That was the tree in which the Great Woodpecker sometimes sits," said Took.

"Oh?"

"One of our great-great-grandfathers accidentally saw it one evening. He went blind, of course."

"Of course. Did he say how big it was?"

"He said that before he went blind, he saw that it sat on the limb, and the top of its head was higher than the top of the tree trunk."

"That's awfully big," I said. I had been expecting something maybe two meters tall.

"Sure is," said Took. He broke into some kind of song. Others took it up, including the Buzzard Cult people.

―――――――――

We watched their fires, and we knew they were watching ours. There was an old flood plain between two small bluffs about half a kilometer apart. We were on one, and the Huastecas were on the other. The battle would take place on the flat place between us tomorrow.

"Better get some sleep," said Took, who had spread his skins out beside mine. We were eating a supper of jerky and ground cornmeal with a few walnuts mixed in. Took passed the waterskin over.

"It could take all day, what with breaks for lunch and stuff," he said.

"Pretty civilized."

"You won't think so if you get caught, or off by yourself, which is the same thing," he said. "Stick close to a mob. If you get caught, they'll probably come get you. Don't let them cover your mouth, whatever you do. Keep yelling."

"Thanks. What really happens?"

"Well, we sort of run together in a big bunch and hit each other, and drag off captives, then eat, then do it some more, and about two hours from sunset we all go home, and three days later we ransom, but that's only chiefman business. Our part will be over. If this were a real battle, we'd take heads instead of captives."

I watched the bright stars overhead through the glow of the fires. It was early spring, and still cool.

I know it was just me, but I had trouble sleeping. Took called out in a dream. He woke up and looked at me.

"My spirit is troubled," he said. He closed his eyes and was asleep again immediately.

"Yee! Yee! Yee!" Yelled Sun Man, facing east. Up and down our bluff, other Sun Men were doing the same thing.

Not that everybody wasn't awake anyway. Men had started moving around long before sunup. I know; I was one of them.

I was sharpening the point of my javelin. I had my own survival knife with me, and was depending on my club, which was about half the size and shape of a Louisville Slugger. I was hoping I wouldn't get close enough to anybody to have to use it.

Sunlight came through a break between the clouds and the horizon. There were pines behind us, where we'd come from, and bayous past that. The land behind the Huastecas was more open. Far to left and right were sparse trees. The flood plain between us was smooth with sand and short grasses. It was about the closest thing to a playing field you could ask for.

After we stuffed our faces, the Sun Men moved around, talking with each other. Our Sun Man came back to us. Some other Sun Man had been elected battle captain.

"Wait for the signal," said Sun Man.

We all filed up on the bluff. A like number of Huastecas faced us across the flat place. They started to rap their spears and clubs against their shields. I could barely make them out — feathered and furred headdresses, copper, maybe gold breastplates and armor. The racket increased, settled into a rhythm — chunk, chunk, chunk. It was my own heartbeat, my pulse. Jeez, those guys knew how to get on your nerves.

The Huastecas hit their shields harder, louder. The booming came like surf across the flood plain, wave after wave.

The Sun Man battle chief raised his arm. We were all quiet, tense. I licked my lips and re-gripped my club.

The Huastecas came down the bluff like a gold and copper waterfall.

"Go get 'em, boys!" said Sun Man.

We took off down the slope, whooping and hollering.

———

Our first hint that something was wrong came when a whole forest of arrows filled the sky from behind the Huasteca bluff.

Those who had them stopped and put their shields over their heads. I climbed under one with three other guys. "Quit shoving!" someone yelled.

The arrows whizzed half a meter into the ground around us, bounced off shields, stuck in people's hands. There were screams.

"Hey, you assholes!" yelled Moe at the Huastecas. "You can't use arrows!"

They were still running toward us, and another rain of arrows came up like a curtain.

Arrows also came from left and right.

"Shit!" yelled Curly.

This time arrows bounced off shields and ricocheted into arms and legs and chests.

"Hell with this!" Larry said; he dropped his spear and unlimbered his ceremonial bow from across his back, stringing it in a swift motion. He put two arrows into the wall of advancing Huastecas.

"They mean business," said Took quietly.

We looked back toward the bluff. The chief Sun Man was jumping up and down pointing to both sides.

It was just like an old Western movie. On three sides of us was a long continual line of Huastecas, with archers behind them. They seemed to have come from nowhere. Arrows sailed up again. The warriors running toward us stopped short, waiting for the arrows to fall on us.

The noise was like hail on a tin roof.

From under the shield with the other guys I saw the second wave of Huastecas start down the bluff — at least twice as many as in the first wave.

"Every man for himself!" yelled Sun Man. "This is death stuff!"

The Buzzard Cultists let out a tremendous yell and sprang out from under their shields straight toward the Huastecas.

Then the Meshicas were on us.

I saw a guy with a jaguar headdress raise a club so I pushed my javelin at him. It went right in. He was as surprised as I was, dropped his club and held his stomach around the spear shaft. He fell down, taking the short spear with him.

Then some sonofabitch hit me in the face with his shield as hard as he could. I didn't have time to think. I was down and all I could see were his feet. So I smashed one of them with my club. He fell on top of me. I tried to get out from under him so he couldn't kill me.

He turned dead weight. I got out from under. Somebody had stuck a javelin in his eye.

I pulled my spear out of the guy it was still sticking in. He gave me a startled look. he was still kneeling and holding his stomach. Guys were fighting all around him. He paid no attention.

I waded into six or eight guys who were fighting and started hitting all the ones with eagle feathers and jaguar skins.

———————

Horns and bugle things were blowing. Drums rattled off in the distance. There were grunts and screams all around. Dust hung in the air. The sun glinted off metal. You couldn't see jack shit.

A spear came at me, got larger, stayed the same, went past me a meter away. I saw the Huasteca who threw it and started for him. Five or six of his buddies came out of nowhere and started for me. Two of them sprouted arrows from their chests.

"Sonofabitches!" said Larry, behind me. He threw down his bow. His quiver was empty. He had time to get his obsidian-studded club out before the four Meshicas got to us.

One of them was covered with armor — breastplate, shin-guards, epaulets. He wore a copper helmet with a long plume, and he had a shield. A *kahuna* of some kind. He came right at me. He took the point of my javelin with his shield and twisted it away. His club came down and knocked the spear from my hands.

Larry's club came across and caved in the front of his helmet. His face looked like something from a Warner Bros. cartoon covered in ketchup.

Somebody got behind Larry and had his hands on his chin. I hit the hands, then Larry's shoulder, then the hands, then farther up with my club. Whoever it was let go and ran off.

A spear butt got me in the head. Blue-green stars covered the tunnel in front of me. I swung. The tunnel went away. Larry was standing on a Huasteca's chest, beating his head as hard as he could.

"Sonofabitch!" said Larry with each blow. "Sonofa-bitch!" We were in a lull. Waves of men were crashing and roaring into each other with tin-can sounds. A horn blew close behind me. I jumped, looked around for my spear, found it.

Larry was through with the guy. He and I stood, heaving and panting, trying to see what was going on in the heat and dust.

Then the second wave of Huastecas ran over us.

I don't know how much later it was when we were back on our bluff. Dust still hung over the flood plain. It was hot. I was so dry my tongue hurt. I could taste blood. I didn't know whether it was mine or someone else's.

Another rain of arrows came out of the dust. "Heads up!" yelled Moe. They sailed into our position, pinning a few guys to the ground.

"Sun damn them all to hell!" said Sun Man. He had been wounded in the side and the arm during the battle. Two of our people were holding him up.

Took was watching across the plain. The dust was beginning to settle. We could see weapons, clothing, drums littering the ground. There were no bodies. We had taken our wounded and dead, and they had taken theirs. They had also taken about fifty prisoners.

We hadn't taken any.

I was getting my breath back. I was covered with grit and dust mixed with sweat, blood, and grease. There were cuts and bruises all over me. There was a wet pain low down on my back. My javelin was a third of a meter shorter than it used to be. My club was gone. My knife was in my hand, dark red.

There were two human heads at my feet.

I didn't remember where they had come from. I didn't remember anything but the endless fighting and the thirst worse than any I had ever had.

The Buzzard Cult people were starting one of their chants.

"Apocalypse stuff," said Took.

"What happened?" I asked.

"The Huastecas have quit playing by the rules."

"Why?"

"I don't know, Yaz. Things are changing. Maybe the Buzzard Cult people are right."

"You better believe we are," said Hamboon Bokulla, the Dreaming Killer, as his people finished their song. "And you better get with it, or be left behind," he said to Took.

Tired, bruised, beaten, we picked up our heads all along the line and started home.

Over the other bluff, the Huastecas were already gone.

———————

Next day, three kilometers or so away from the village, I realized what I had done.

We were passing a small creek. Our wounded were leaning on other warriors. Almost everybody was gimped up in some way. I walked to the creek and stood on its bank.

One after the other, I threw the heads as far as I could downstream. The last one's eyes stayed on me in its flight toward the water as if it were a ballerina and I were its turning point. *Guilty, guilty,* the air whistling past the head said. It hit with a splash a few meters behind the first and sank immediately.

"You shouldn't have done that," said Took, standing behind me.

"Why not?" I asked.

"They were pretty good heads," he said, and rejoined the struggling file of the Woodpecker people.

the box

8

DA FORM 1   1 52 1 Z   11NOV 2002

COMP __147__   TOE ____148____

PRES FOR DUTY: 142
KILLED IN ACTION   3
KILLED LINE OF DUTY   1
MISSING LINE OF DUTY   1

TOTAL: 147

FOR: S. SPAULDING   BY: BARNES, BONNIE
       COL, INF.   CPT, ADC
       COMMANDING   ADJUTANT

AFP 907-11M-996

DA FORM 1

1402 Z 2 DEC 2002

COMP 147   TOE 148

PRES FOR DUTY:	131
KIA	7
KLD	2
MIA	6
MLD	1

TOTAL: 147

FOR: 3.SPAULDING
COL, INF.
COMMANDING

BY: BARNES, BONNIE
CPT, ADC
ADJUTANT

AFP 907-11M-996

DA FORM 1   1702 Z   24 DECEMBER 2002

COMP 147   TOE 148

PRES FOR DUTY: 111
KIA   13
KLD   2
MIA   11
MLD   1
WOUNDED, HOSPITAL 9
TOTAL: 147

FOR: S. SPAULDING   BY: BARNES, BONNIE

COL. INF.   CPT, ADC
COMMANDING   ADJUTANT

AFP 907-11M-996

Smith's Diary   December 24 (Christmas Eve)

Today we sent out an eleven-man patrol to try to reach the location of Baton Rouge and go far south from there, the only direction we haven't tried.

I don't know what they're supposed to find. Help. Frenchmen. Some of de Soto's conquistadors. Ponce de Leon? Maybe they can convince some other Indians to help us, or get a treaty with the ones we are warring with.

They continue to snipe at us. Two more wounded today, in spite of the bunkers. I never knew arrows could carry so far — they send them up out of the woods; you can't see where they come from. By the time you see the arrow, it's on the way down. You duck for cover, trampling over everybody else. One of the wounded today was already down flat, behind the bunker wall, against the sandbags, and the arrow came down straight and stuck him to the ground like a pin through a beetle. Fortunately, it only got him through the meaty part of the thigh.

Private Dorothy Jones wasn't so lucky — she got one straight in the ribs, this one fired from the nearest clump of brush about a hundred meters away.

We returned fire in both cases. In the first, we laced the area where the arrow came from with small arms and LMG fire. We won't know what happened there till we send out the usual patrol.

We do know what happened with the second. As soon as Jones was hit, two of the bunkers cranked up. They fired about 200 rounds each into the bushes the arrow was shot from, tearing them flat, destroying small trees and the ground.

When they stopped, an Indian stood up, dropped his breechcloth and mooned us, then jumped back flat to the ground.

Major Putnam ordered the heavy machine guns to cease fire after another minute. The target area was unrecognizable. There was nothing more than a few centimeters high in the beaten zone. It was like a photograph retouched by a clumsy person, like a picture of the woods with a blank swath taken out.

The Indian jumped up out of the middle of it and ran into the woods.

Putnam wouldn't let anybody fire.

Spaulding, who fought in Cyprus, says there could be two Indians a day sniping at us, or a hundred, and we'll never know.

The eleven-man patrol left at dawn after we laid down some grenades in the direction they'd travel. It must have been okay: we didn't hear any shooting.

They reported in okay three hours later over the radio. They were twenty klicks south and had seen nobody. They would report every two hours. Not that we could help if they needed it. They had all volunteered.

Meanwhile, we're all digging in further. Arrows go through tents. We can't cut wood. So we're digging in, like moles, making ourselves at home.

There are important things we should be doing, somewhere, sometime. Here we're useless. We should be changing the world, not hiding from people with bows and arrows and spears.

We didn't mean to kill them. It wasn't our fault. We took precautions against bringing any diseases back with us.

The medic says it's probably something we only notice as a sniffle or a sore throat. To them it's death in two days flat.

We tried to help, to let them know we're sorry. They just don't understand.

Meanwhile, while we dig, we have music. I find my body moving to the rocking rhythm of Roger Whitaker. We've been here too long.

There was a new sound on the River.

Part metallic clang, part wooden knock, it came from the bend of the River.

Guys with conch shells on the lookout mounds began to blow them. Everyone took off for the canoe landing.

Took was in the hut. Sunflower came around from the garden patch. She brushed dirt from her hands.

Sun Man and a delegation stopped outside Took's hut.

"The ones on the River are the ones you want to see," Took said to me.

L E A K E 9

He stood, pulled on a bright feather mantle, then picked up the rolled bag of pipes he had been working on all winter.

I went out with him, stood behind some of the minor nobles, then we all walked through the village, out the river gate and down toward the water.

Half the village was standing and waiting there already. A plume of smoke rose up through the trees downriver. I felt we were in the old Currier and Ives print, "Waiting on the Levee."

It *appeared* around the bend.

It had been so long since I'd seen any machinery I'd almost forgotten what it was like. The prow appeared, broad, flat and low. The front of the second deck, then the third. All painted bright red with yellow stripes like a hot dog covered with mustard. There were tall fair figures on the deck.

They had horns.

There was the long blast of a whistle, then the roar of a foghorn. The people onshore jumped and held their ears. The ship turned in toward the canoe landing, the figure on the prow casting a plumbline again and again before him.

> "Antiquity held too light thoughts from Objects of mortality, while some drew provocatives of mirth from Anatomies, and jugglers shewed tricks with Skeletons."
> — Browne, *Urn Burial*

The craft had two paddlewheels amidships. Above the upper deck flew a pennon with a red scimitar on a white field.

The figures in the pilothouse wore bright red robes and turbans.

There was another blast on the horn and a long release of steam from somewhere amidships. The paddles stopped, reversed, backed water. The ship, as big as the temple mound, slid quietly into the landing, as stately as a hotel.

The front of the ship, a drawbridge-type ramp, arched over slowly and jerked down to the ground of the bank. There was another piercing whistle and the people of the village began to cheer.

A short man in a robe and turban, followed by others dressed in robes or leather pants and jerkins, carrying arquebuses and blunderbusses, stepped to the top of the ramp.

"Took, my old friend," he said in Greek. "Tell Sun Man and your people hello and that we come to trade, even up, sky is the limit, for whatever and how much?"

Took turned to the people, nodded to Sun Man, made a short speech.

The people yelled wildly, jumped around, began laying their wares, skins, weapons art and food out onto their blankets on the ground.

The men came down the planks, all smiles, holding their hands out to hug Took, and bow to Sun Man. The deckhands, some in loose pants and fezes, others in their horned and beaked helmets, began unloading the trade goods of the ship into the open area above the landing.

"This," said Took, "is Aroun el Hama, king of merchants."

"And this," he continued, "is Madison Yazoo Leake."

"Hello," I said in Greek.

He looked at me. He was small, with hard dark eyes, a coal-black beard and salt and pepper mustache. A small scar went from his left eyebrow to his missing left earlobe.

"By Ibram," he said, "are you a southerner gone wild on us?"

"No," I said, "much farther away than that, I fear."

"Your accent," said el Hama. "You learned the language nowhere I know."

"I'm sure you two will want to talk tonight," said Took. "Aroun, they're going to kill us all if we don't get some trading done." People were yelling and pointing to their goods all up and down the landing.

"Yaz," said Took. "Give us a hand, will you?" He pointed over to where one of the guys with a horned helmet was arguing in one language with a village woman arguing in another.

I went over to help. It took a while, what with my trouble with the moundbuilder language, and the accent of the northerner, a big red-headed dude, to find that they had argued the price both up and down and had passed the price they had both agreed to long before.

It was going to be a long hot day.

the box

9

DA FORM 1 <u>1614 **Z** 01 JAN 2 00 3</u>

COMP <u>147</u>   TOE <u>148</u>

PRES FOR DUTY: <u>115</u>
KILLED IN ACTION   13
KILLED LINE OF DUTY   <u>3</u>
MISSING IN ACTION   <u>11</u>
MISSING LINE OF DUTY   1
WOUNDED, HOSPITAL   4
TOTAL: <u>147</u>

FOR: <u>S.SPAULDING</u>   BY: <u>ATWATER, WILLEY</u>

<u>COLONEL, INFANTRY</u>   <u>2LT, ARM.</u>

<u>COMMANDING</u>   <u>ACT. ADJ.</u>

AFP 907-11M-996

The day was overcast, humid and hot, and it was just dawn.

Bessie sketched the depressions around the mounds. There were there on the flood terrace, one west, one north, one east-northeast. She drew in the bluff line. The mounds occupied the center. There were shallower areas around them. She flipped over the pages of her field book. Perhaps this had been a village site? But they'd found no post molds yet, no typical village structures. Maybe it had been a temporary habitation site, used only while the mounds were being raised.

Perch and the others arrived with the muddy sun. This time Perch was in work clothes, his tiny frame lost inside them.

They waited for him to get out of his car. Over at the trucks, the photographer and artists were getting out their equipment. Down below, the work crews were taking off the tarps from the mounds.

"Governor's still not back," said Perch. "Won't be for two, three days. There seems to be a small mutiny in his party machine. Also" — he looked down at the bayou — "we're in for rain, lots of it. They've closed the gates downstream and opened the ones above. It's raining like hell in Shreveport, and all up the Mississippi. They think this one might be as bad as the spring flood two years ago. I figure we got five, maybe six days."

"What about a coffer dam?" asked Kincaid.

"We can use part of the crews to work on it. I've sent to the University for maintenance crews with some tractors. I tried to get a hold of the highway department, but nobody's doing anything until the governor gets back and they see who's on top."

"That's probably why he left," said Jameson. "Giving 'em enough rope."

"That's why nobody's answering their phones," said Perch.

B

E

S

S

I

E

7

"Where do we put the dam?" asked Kincaid. He opened the survey map. "Along the line of the old terrace?"

"That's way too big," said Jameson. "We're going to have to decide whether we save Mound One or not. I say no."

"Bessie?" asked Perch.

She looked at the far mound, totally typical, left unopened and alone with its grid markers. "We can't take a chance on losing Two A and Two B," she said. "Oh, hell, what if it's just as full of stuff as this one?"

"Kincaid?"

"Oh, hell with it. Put the dam here, just below Two A. Bring it back around to the bluff on each side, maybe dig drainage over here, if we can."

Bessie looked at the grid map.

"Dr. Perch, can we bring it out another ten feet, over here?" She pointed past the east-northeast shallow depression. "If we've got time, I want to dig here." She stabbed the map with her finger.

"We don't have time," said Jameson.

She told them about Basket and the flood legend.

They all looked at the shallow spots. "They could be nothing but borrow pits," Perch said. "That what you want to save?"

She had a moment of uncertainty. "Yes, I do."

"Call up the crews," said Perch. "The three of you get down there, go straight in and down on the mound. Find out what happened there. I haven't been out in the woods for a long time, but I still know how to make dams."

They had the dam outlined and shovels started to fly.

In the platform of Mound Two B, they found the first of the human skeletons by midmorning.

It lay, feet outward, directly below the test trench. William found the feet, and called Kincaid over. Slowly they removed dirt from the bones, to the pelvis, the ribcage, the shoulders.

There was no skull. The neck ended abruptly.

Kincaid dug to the right and left.

"Bessie," he said, "get the shellac and come in behind me and coat the skeleton. We'll leave it *in situ*. It's brittle. There wasn't any covering; this skeleton was just lain on the original ground line and the mound raised over it."

Bessie dolloped thick gobs of shellac onto the paper-soft bones, then slowly spread it with a fine brush.

"Look at this," said Kincaid.

The left arm of another skeleton lay exposed to the right of the first.

"Right about there, I'd say," said Bessie, pointing to the left of the first skeleton she worked on, "and up a little."

"Just what I was thinking," said Kincaid. He began to dig where she had pointed. Soon he had the right arm bones of another skeleton exposed to view.

"Jameson," he called softly.

Jameson came around from his work on the other side of the mound's test trench. He had his hat off, but his eyes were bright like a squirrel's. He smiled.

"It's a trophy mound, isn't it?" said Jameson.

"I think so," said Kincaid. "I surely do think so. How many skulls have you found yet?"

"None. They don't have heads."

They both looked up at the conical burial mound which sat atop the platform mound. It was untouched as yet, except for the two-foot profile cut.

"I vote we go in there," said Bessie.

"Get the photographer and artist down there on those skeletons," said Kincaid.

Thunder rumbled. "Shit!" said Jameson.

the box

10

Smith's Diary   January 4 — the new year

I was talking with Colonel Spaulding in his bunker.

"When I was a boy," he said, taking a book out of his personal locker, "this book was it." It was The Book of Mormon.

"You were raised a Mormon?"

"The Church of Jesus Christ of the Latter Day Saints," he said, almost automatically. "I still do that, listen to me. And I haven't been to services in thirty years."

"Yes, sir?"

"Well, you've probably never read it," he said. "Most people never have, never will. But parts of it keep coming back to me.

"See, there are a couple of narratives within narratives. It took me a long time to realize that as a kid. The golden plates were supposedly found at Cumorah, but they also recapitulate earlier records also buried there, from an even earlier time."

"Yes?"

"Well, the earliest migration involved prophets who sailed from Jerusalem and came to America. They built great cities here, but fell to fighting among themselves. They divided into the Lamanites and the Jaredites. The Lamanites were punished, their skins turned red, and all their cities fell to waste and ruin."

"Those are the Indians?"

Spaulding laughed. "I know, sounds like the old Ten Lost Tribes of Israel, or lost Phoenicians, or Egyptians, doesn't it? When I was a kid, I was hot on archeology. But I've forgotten most of it, like I thought I'd forgotten most of The Book of Mormon. Seems some stuck with me, though."

"It would be a lot easier if it were true," I said. "Maybe Arnstein can go speak with them?"

Spaulding laughed, a different tone. "From what I remember, those theories about lost Romans and such came about because the early white settlers who found the mounds and earthworks couldn't believe the Indians had built them. The only Indians they knew were the ones still in the area, who hadn't moved there in many cases until fifty years before the whites got there. The Indians didn't know where the mounds came from, either. So the settlers thought they predated the Indians themselves. And were a much more advanced civilization than the Indians could have had.

"So they searched around for examples of Old World civilizations who had ever used mounds and high fortifications. That was nearly everybody, of course — Welsh, Mongol, Roman, Egyptian, all of them came in for their turn as the original Mound-builders."

"These people we're fighting are certainly better at warfare than we thought they would be," I said.

"The old adage is that primitive doesn't mean stupid," said Colonel Spaulding.

"Shooting at us is one thing," I said. "But I think it was the radio business that really upset everybody."

"Well, we deserve it," said Spaulding, with an anger I didn't know he had. "We've disrupted their lives. We killed them as surely as if we'd held weapons to their heads. They can't understand we didn't want it to happen." He went quiet, staring down at his desk.

"We've seen enough killing. We've seen the whole world killed. Now we're killing the past, too. None of us wanted this, least of all the Indians." He picked up The Book of Mormon again, opened it.

I stood up. "I'd better check the guard."

"Certainly, Marie," he said. "Send Putnam over here, will you?"

I saluted and left. Sometimes Spaulding was hard to figure out.

I never saw so much stuff traded in my life. Skins, furs, food, shells, art and pipes went into the ship, and out came beads, knives, tools, cloth, copper, and brass.

I helped as much as I could, going from one haggle to another. There seemed to be no set price for anything on either side. I kept busy, and watched the interaction of the merchants and the people of the village.

The Northerners spoke Greek as badly accented as my own. The turbaned merchants spoke Asiatic Greek, a lot like that of the Turkish Cypriots. But strange things had happened to it — idioms were lost on me, lots of references to arid lands, deserts, but also whales and ice-cold water.

They had their own translators who spoke a down-river or crossriver speech, Indians who dressed half merchant, half local. There was lots of gesturing, some common signs and symbols, much body language.

The whole thing was like a refresher course at the Tower of Babel.

Somehow things got traded and commerce went on. I looked to the boat and saw a merchant come out and shoot the sun with a sextant, all brass and enamel.

Sun Man looked up. "Noon," he said.

In the middle of the afternoon, the whistle on the ship blew and everybody picked up their goods and went back into the village or the ship.

**L
E
A
K
E

10**

Aroun el Hama and merchants and Northerners accompanied us back to the huts.

Took got into step beside me.

"We'll feast them in the village, then they'll feast us on the ship tonight. There'll be a little trading tomorrow. Then

"Man is a noble animal, splendid in ashes,
pompous in the grave."
— Browne, *Urn Burial*

they'll trade upriver and hit us back on the way down in a moon or so."

The fun was already starting. People were tapping on drums and tootling on flutes. One of the merchants had a guitar-looking thing with only five strings.

About a third of the way to the plaza, my horse whinnied over in its pen.

The merchants froze as stiff as Larry, Curly, and Moe had the first time they heard it.

"I must have trading fever," said el Hama. "I thought I heard a horse."

"You did," I said. "It's mine."

For a moment I thought he was going to cry.

"Could we see it?" he asked.

I led them to it. El Hama and the others gentled it down, then began patting it and talking excitedly in Arabic.

"We have brought no horses to these shores yet," said el Hama. "Though they plan to begin trading them soon, up around the Eastern Ocean. Where did you get such an animal?"

"It's a long story," I said. "I have thousands of things to ask you, but they can wait. Would you like to ride him?"

"All I have is yours," he said, bowing.

I put the bridle on the horse. El Hama sprang up on his back with the grace of a man half his age.

I opened the pen. El Hama guided the horse out onto the plaza to the cheers of the onlookers, put it into an easy canter. Then he turned it, brought it back to where we stood.

"So that's what you do with it!" said Sun Man. "Someday, Yazoo, you will have to teach me to do that."

El Hama took the horse a few more trips around the plaza, then reluctantly came back. He knew he was holding up his hosts.

"He rides beautifully," he said, dismounting. "Ah, it will be fine when such animals as this live in this land." He looked at me. "You will dine with us this night aboard the ship?"

"Certainly."

"I also have questions to ask you. Many, many questions," he said.

We had reached Sun Man's house. People started handing us food and drink, and trying to get us to dance.

The platform mound looked like a pie graph. The test trench led in from each side, widened out in wedges where the headless skeletons had been uncovered on each side.

Jameson, Kincaid, and Bessie were opening the conical mound atop the other.

"We'd better work in from this side."

"We're going to have to take this whole mound system down to ground level, starting with the top."

"Is that what I think it is? Give me that whisk broom."

"Look at that."

"There's another one under it."

"Over here, too."

"I'll bet these just fit some of the necks downstairs."

"You know they do."

"Still more. What that thunder again?"

"Hell yes! Washington! Tear down my tent and bring it down here. Put all my stuff in the sorting room."

"How's the dam?"

"I can't see anything from here."

"Oh boy."

"What?"

"See those mold marks?"

"Everybody out! Get the photographer in here. You getting this profile, Bessie?"

"More skulls down here. God knows how many. That means a lot of skeletons down below, probably. These skulls must be piled up from the level of the top of the platform mound."

"And this mound has different soil..."

"Look, look."

"Part of a log tomb?"

"Has to be, has to be."

**B
E
S
S
I
E

8**

"Get more light in here."

"It's darker outside."

"Must be storming again. This tent's going to take off."

"I hope they got the other tarps back down. Who's shellacking?"

"Leroy!"

"Good."

"Find me something about a quarter inch thick and ten inches long."

———————

"Get the photographer in here! Bring the shellac!"

———————

"Is that rain again?"

———————

"God! This guy must have been the Rockefeller of his time."

"Ignore all that stuff right now. Look at the arm."

"Broken and regrown."

"But look at that nick on the bone!"

"Get the photographer in here!"

———————

"Easy, easy. Try to brush — there. Let me have the ice pick. No. The curved one. There. Wait. Wait."

"What are those?"

"Try to keep the head attached."

"I can't do very much of anything with that damn breastplate in the way."

"Can you keep them in one piece?"

"Maybe."

"That's steel."

"Maybe."

"I've got it. Them. And the head's still on."

"Get them back to the sorting tent. Is that rain again?"

———————

Bessie walked with the object cupped in her hands. It was a necklace made of tiny metal beads. Attached to it through holes drilled in their edges were many dozen thin rusted oblongs of metal, one inch wide, two inches long.

On at least one was writing in English.

Dawn was breaking, wet and sodden. They had been at work on the mound for twenty hours.

the box

11

DA FORM 1   1524 Z 3 FEB 2003

COMP 147   TOE 148

PRES FOR DUTY: 106

KIA   13

KLD   4

MIA   12

MLD   1

WOUNDED, HOSP   11

TOTAL: 147

FOR: SPAULDING, S.   BY: ATWATER, W.

COL, INF   2LT, ARM.

COM   ACTING ADJ

AFP 907-11M-996

DA FORM 1
<u>172 1 Z   6-MARCH-03</u>

COMP <u>147</u>   TOE <u>148</u>

PRES FOR DUTY:	91
KIA	22
KLD	6
MIA	21
MLD	1
WOUNDED, HOSP	6

TOTAL: <u>147</u>

FOR: <u>S. SPAULDING</u>   BY: <u>ATWATER, WILLEY</u>

<u>COL, INF</u>   <u>1LT, ARM.</u>

<u>COMMANDING</u>   <u>ACTING ADJ</u>

AFP 907-11M-996

DA FORM 1 <u>2014 Z 11 APR 2003</u>

COMP <u>147</u>   TOE <u>148</u>

PRES FOR DUTY: <u>81</u>
KIA   <u>23</u>
KLD   <u>6</u>
MIA   <u>21</u>
MLD   <u>1</u>
WOUNDED, HOSP   <u>15</u>

TOTAL: <u>147</u>

FOR: <u>S. SPAULDING</u>   BY: <u>ATWATER, WILLEY</u>

<u>COL, INF</u>   <u>1LT, ARM</u>

<u>COMMANDING</u>   <u>ACTING ADJ</u>

AFP 907-11M-996

WAR DEPARTMENT

20 July 1929

RE: Serial Nos Possible
    US Army Personnel

Dr. Kincaid
Salvage Survey
c/o Dixie Hotel
Suckatoncha, Louisiana
via Baton Rouge

Dr. Kincaid:

In re: list of 75 possible US Army
personnel your communication
18 July 1929. Two (2) names match
current active duty US Army
personnel, one duty Philippine
Islands, one assigned Ft. Meade
Maryland, officer rank not NCO.
DOBs do not match.

Check underway US Navy & Marine
Corps. Message relayed DOTreasury
for Coast Guard personnel.
DOInterior Veteran's Bureau
checking, answer expected NLT COB
this date. Will forward Daughters
Confederacy, S-A War Veterans.

Expect arrival your area ASAP
Cpt Thompson, Graves Registration
Officer this command to assist,
act as liaison govt. agencies this
problem.

Jillam, T.V.
Cpt, Art.
Acting Asst AGC

B
E
S
S
I
E

9

We had to quit eating late in the afternoon. We waddled back to our huts and lay down and went to sleep.

Just at dark we were wakened by the whistle of the ship.

Took and I, Sun Man, some of the nobles, several warriors, and a couple of the artisans had been invited to the boat. The only Buzzard Cult person there was Moe, who was also head of one of the kinship systems.

We all met at the landing. The ship was dark. Then, all at once, it lit up with a cool blue light like giant glowworms were inside the decks and passageways.

L E A K E

11

El Hama and his men came down to greet us and led us aboard. They seated us around the largest room, maybe a third the length of the ship, on the second deck.

We ate again, while three of the merchants played on a guitar, drum, and flute. Several of the Northerners did acrobatics for us, like great bears inside their shaggy skins. I was seated on the opposite side of the circle from Took, Sun Man, and el Hama. I followed the conversation as best I could. It was mostly of inconsequentialities, trade, hunting, weather, crops, the surplus of skins and the shortage of bear's teeth, and (el Hama begged pardon) woodpecker scalps. It was a lot like my idea of what a Rotary Club lunch in Des Plaines on a slow Tuesday would be like.

Then they brought coffee.

I thought I was going to die. I knew what it was before I saw it; I smelled it first. I had not had any since my last pack of instant went into the canteen cup two weeks after I got here, months ago.

> "But remembering the early civilitie they brought upon these countreys, and forgetting long passed mischiefs, we mercifully preserve their bones and pisse not upon their ashes."
> — Browne, *Urn Burial*

Took's people drink several teas and herb drinks, mostly when it's cold or they're under the weather. Some of them, like sassafras and cedar bark, are good. But they're not coffee.

I stared at the elaborate double urn like it was a metal god.

El Hama said something to Took, watching me all the while.

They served the coffee in a way as elaborate as any Japanese tea ceremony. The water in the lower part of the urn was boiling hot. One of the merchants poured a kilo of dark coffee grounds into the top urn, then put what looked like powdered milk and a half kilo of fructose in with it. Putting another urn under that, he dashed the boiling water into the upper pot.

The smell took me to heaven and back again. A minute later he pulled out the lower pot. It was filled to overflowing with a brown cloud-like froth.

"Now quickly," said el Hama to all present, "we must drink while the face is still on the coffee." Tiny cups filled with a small amount of liquid were handed, with the right hand, to the right. The cups foamed with a head of cream, sugar and puffed coffee. It was all I could do to keep handing the cups around the circle, instead of drinking them all up as they got to me.

At last, everybody had one, Sun Man being the last. Then the circle filled back to me. My cup, they handed me my cup!

When everyone had one, they all looked at el Hama. He took a tiny sip of the coffee head, rolled his eyes, put the cup back in his saucer. Disappointed, they took tiny sips also.

I wanted to gulp mine down, start a fight, take everybody's cup away from them. I sipped mine instead.

It was wonderful, but it was only semisweet, and filled with cream. What I wanted was about two liters of coffee with a half kilo of sugar in it. I wanted a caffeine rush that would bring Dwight Eisenhower back to life.

I could hear coffee dripping into the pot, now ignored.

Sometime during the low talk which followed, Took came around the circle to me.

"El Hama wants to see you afterwards. In the general milling around, go through the passageway to the right, and out onto the aft deck and wait for him there. I'll see you in the morning."

I nodded.

Soon there was a giving around of presents, at which I got a bird whistle necklace. The bird was made of something like a cross between hard rubber and anthracite coal. It made a sound like one of those tweeting Christmas tree ornaments when I tried it. I put it on around my neck.

There *was* general milling around. I went out the right doorway, up a blue-lit passage. There was a guard at the far doorway, a Northerner, who only nodded as I neared him, and I went by.

The blue lights had a faint buzz, like neon. Electricity. In one room off the passageway I saw a clerk writing in a big ledger by the light of an oil lamp. He paid no attention to me, and I went out up onto the deck.

The night was dark; there was no moon yet. The next was the planting moon, time of the Black Drink ceremony Took had mentioned, after the crops were put down. It was supposedly only March here, by my reckoning, but it was already warm.

The upper deck of the boat loomed above me, the light in the pilot house a blue box against the starry sky. There were a few crewmen on deck, a few Northerners or Arabs. One was fishing off the lower deck with a long pole.

The first bullfrogs of spring were croaking. I heard an alligator grunt. The palisade of the village was a darker blot on the sky, with a few firelights showing through the mud chinking.

I had forgotten how big the River was, how full of sounds it was at night, how many mammals, birds, fish, and insects made noises. It all came back to me on the deck of the ship.

Even with the blue lights around me, the Milky Way was a slather of white across the sky, and the stars shone with round flickering brilliance on the darkness.

"Ah," said el Hama as he came on deck, "let's sit near the stern." Pillows were brought out and we sat ourselves down. "More coffee?" he asked.

I could have kissed him.

"I have already sent for it," he said, smiling. "I noticed how much you enjoyed it. And now, we have many questions of each other?"

"Too many, I think," I said.

"And I. Please begin, for I am host tonight."

"What year is this?"

"By our calendar," he said, "it is the 1364th year since the capture of Mecca by the followers of Ibram the Prophet."

Mecca checks out. Who's the prophet Ibram? 1364? All the Islamic turmoil was in what, the 600s? This is what? Late 1900s? Maybe even 2000 AD?

"Do you know of one named Mohammed?" I asked.

"The father of the Prophet? Not much is written of him in the Book."

"Uh, what about Jesus?"

"I am not as much of a scholar as our physician — Send for Ali," he said to another merchant, then turned back to me. "Jesus? I think he was worshipped near Galilee, a small sect perhaps? I think he was stoned by his people. The Prophet lived near Galilee for some months during his exile, I think, when he was cast out of Medina."

Another man came out, bringing his own pillow, and seated himself next to us. He was introduced to me as Ali the physician.

"He asks of people mentioned in the Book," said el Hama, "but he asks strangely."

I sighed. "What about Egypt?"

"The mother of all nations," said el Hama. "Old before the stone fell from the sky at Qabba."

"Well, that's a start. We share that. What of Greece, Athens, Sparta?"

"Seats of learning and manliness," said Ali. "Lightgiver and conquering state, of unparalleled achievements, whose glory lasted for centuries. You speak its language."

"What of the Romans and their Empire?"

"Who?" asked el Hama.

"I *have* heard of them," said Ali, shifting his spectacles.

"They were barely mentioned in the histories. They were city dwellers who made war on their neighbors and conquered their peninsula. They fought mother Carthage. Twice, I think."

"What happened to them?"

"The second time, Carthage, who only wanted free trade with all her neighbors, defeated these Romans and all their allies. I am told they made wonderful shepherds and farmers."

"So there was no Roman Empire?"

"An empire of wool," said Ali. "We trade dearly for it."

"And Carthage?"

"Oh, mother Carthage is still there. Only a minor seaport now. It was captured in the eighteenth year after the Prophet's death. And all Africa north of the River Congo."

"What of Europe? The Church?"

"Europe?"

"The land north of the Mediterranean west of the Bosporus. Uh, Dardanelles."

"Oh. A land of barbarians. The True Religion of the Prophet took it wholly and easily. What parts the Northerners did not already hold."

"What did you do when you met with them?"

"We offered them forty percent," said el Hama. "They were great sailors and navigators. They knew the lands of the north from raiding them so often. One of them had already traveled to this land when the True Religion spread over the north."

"But there was so much land there," said Ali, "so much produce and trade that our merchants thought of coming here again only thirty years or so ago, when we developed power enough to make the journey easily. And now we have this whole new world of trade to manage."

"It seems too simple," I said. "Was there a Great Plague? Did the followers of the True Religion put the people whom they conquered to the fire and sword?"

"Plague? There are always plagues of one kind or another," said Ali. "Little can be done with them. But a great plague, no. Hippocrates says that nations and cities must reach a certain size before the plagues become endemic. We have very few truly large cities."

"You kept Greek learning, then? What about all the lost books? What about the library at Alexandria? Weren't all the books burned?"

"Burn all those great works! What a horrid idea!" said Ali. "But where is this place Alexandria? The great library is in Cairo, in Egypt."

"Alexander the Great? Philip of Macedon? Darius the Persian?" I said.

"These names are unknown to me," said Ali. "Hamilcar established the great library at Cairo. Through the many contacts of Carthage's trade network, he had books brought there. They were there when the True Believers took the city. There they remain, though they have been endlessly recopied, and, I am afraid, many errors have crept into them."

"Then this ship," I said, "the lights? These are all applications of Greek science?"

"Well, yes," said el Hama. "That, and knowledge of our own, through many centuries of experiment and change."

I drank my coffee.

"This will take some getting used to. You say it was thirty years ago your ships first came here?"

"Oh, they'd been coming, one or two at a time, for centuries, by mistake or accident or foolhardy venturing. Sail was fine for the Indian Sea, or what you call the Mediterranean, or northern coastal trade, and West Africa. But for this western trade, you need something you can depend on. Steam. So it was only after we had dependable steam that the Consulate of Merchants sent trading expeditions here."

"And Took-His-Time was captured twenty years ago by one of them? Which is why he speaks Greek?"

"What can I say?" El Hama spread his arms. "As with all frontier operations there were unscrupulous things done in the name of commerce. Many of the unregulated traders carried out similar actions to gain advantage. Take young people, hold them in virtual slavery, use them as interpreters and so on."

"What is this place like, the whole continent, now?"

"I'm sure Took has told you as much as we know. In the northeast, small hunting, fishing, farming groups. In the south — your east — are the mound-builders, like Took and his people. They go from the southeastern peninsula to just west of the Big River we are on. To the northwest, people poorer than the poorest nomads of the deserts of Egypt, a few of whom were brought back to our lands as curiosities by the unprincipled.

"To your west, and southwest for a long way, is the country of the Huastecas. They are the meanest people we have met in this world, though they have a culture nearer to ours. We have a few trade stations to the south, but we really don't like to deal with them much. Neither do your people. But they make such fine jewelry."

"And you trade up and down the River each spring?"

"That is my mission now, though there will soon be others. The trade is so profitable, on both sides, that there is plenty for all, and the trade is so novel to each side that it will remain so. Other markets change, prices come and go. I'm told that right now you can burn cotton in Africa before you can give it away. But bring knives to the New Lands, or take furs back to Egypt, and your market finds itself."

"Yet you restrict your trade in certain ways."

"You speak of firearms, explosives, certain animals?"

"Yes."

"Not through lack of profit, I assure you. But the Consulate of Merchants learned a great lesson in western Africa. Within twenty years of unlimited trade there, we were fighting ten wars, caring for thousands of refugees, and looking at denuded lands unfit for anything. The place had become desert, which year by year creeps farther into the jungle. That was six centuries ago, and we now know better than to do it again."

"That is why we were so surprised to see your horse," said Ali. "It is, as far as we know, the only one on the continent. If it is the only one, there will never be more."

This was the first time they had come around to a question for me. I prefaced my story by saying I didn't understand all that had happened, and certainly didn't expect them to.

I told them what had happened in the world I came from as best as I could remember my history. I told them of Alexander, of Rome, of the rise of Islam (with the father of their Prophet as its leader), of Christianity, and of a Europe at first united then split by religion, of plague, wars, of science, everything I could think of.

The more I told, the more it began to sound to me like a story of greed, folly and misfortune, like a tale told by a crazed and vindictive storyteller with a grudge against humanity.

I told them of that last, terrible war, of the death and dying, and of that last valiant attempt, of which I had been a part, to change all the terrible things that led to the war.

When I finished, I thought they were going to applaud. Their faces were a little sad, but awed, as if I were an entertainer with a trick that had outdone all others they had ever seen.

"Allah works with each of us in His own way," said Ali the physician.

"Come back with us!" said el Hama, suddenly. "There is a man they tell of in Baghdad who appeared one day years ago with a tale such as yours. He is dead now, but some of the learned who talked with him are still alive. Come back with us to the lands of learning, and speak with them."

"I doubt I could do anything but confuse them," I said. "Your invitation is tempting. Ask me again when you come back downriver. I'll think about it till then."

I wondered if others in the Project had been tossed into this world. Or were there others from somewhere else, some other time than mine, or from the future or past of this world, or yet another?

I was tired. My mind could hold only so many things in it. I had reached my limit on novelty and culture shock.

False dawn tinged the sky over the River.

"You have been very helpful," I said. "I don't know how to thank you enough."

"If you wish to go with us when we return, you are welcome," said el Hama. He shook both my hands with his. "We will return halfway through the next moon awash to the line with goods. And perhaps we can ride your horse again? One gets so tired of the ship."

"At any time," I said. "Thank you. And thank you, Ali."

"Take this when you go," said el Hama. One of the Northerners handed me a three-kilo bag of ground coffee.

I felt like crying as I left — for myself, for losing my way, for ending up in this other, crazy world, for mankind. For the coffee. It was all too much.

As they let the ramp down for me to get ashore, I heard one of the Northerners sneeze.

WAR DEPARTMENT

21 July 1929

RE: Serial Nos Possible
    US Army Personnel,
    yours 18 July 1929

Kincaid
Salvage Survey
c/o Dixie Hotel
Suckatoncha, Louisiana
via Baton Rouge

Dr. Kincaid:

US DOInterior Veteran's Bureau
lists three names: one Mexican War
died active duty Nevada Territory
1852, two GAR veterans one died
April 1872 Abrams Massachusettes,
one Old Soldier's Home Seip Va.
DOBs do not match in any case.
List w/ particulars sent via US
Mail.

Daughters Confederacy, SA War
Veterans, Navy-Marine Corps
DOTreasury searches not yet
completed.

ETA Cpt Thompson, this command,
NLT 2200 this date Hotel Dixie.

Jillam,
Act. Asst AGC

**B
E
S
S
I
E

10**

the box

12

Smith's Diary   April 12

*They brought Lewisohn and nine of the people
who went out on the mission four months ago to the
edge of the clearing this morning just after dawn. Their
hands were bound behind them, and they were in bad
shape.*

*The Indians killed them by cutting their throats from
behind, using their bodies for shields as they got back
to cover.*

*We couldn't do anything. Someone ripped off a
clip, but that only made one of the Indians drop a
soldier's body.*

*The rest they took to cover. We don't know what
they did to them. Some of them were still thrashing and
bleeding to death as they dragged them back into
the woods.*

*At first light this morning, the body they had
dropped was gone.*

*Everyone is in a silent rage, which is just what the
Indians want.*

I don't want to write any more for a while.

The messenger came into the village through the growing cornstalks, bringing the first written words I had seen in five months.

He carried a piece of papyrus in a split stick. Took had the messenger sit down, and Sunflower filled him up with fresh squirrel stew. He was from three villages upriver and was anxious to get back.

I opened the paper, but had to strain to figure out some of the writing. It was Greek but with flourishes; a few words I had to guess at.

```
L
E
A
K
E

12
```

Friend Yazoo, [it began]

We of the Trading Companions send you warm greetings. Business, the Prophet bless us, is better than ever.

We shall return downriver in less than a moon's turning, and hope to see you then.

We ask you that you tell Sun Man and all your people to be on their guard. [Something] *is unrest to the west of the River. The tiger-people* [their name for the Huastecas, Took told me] *have been seen more frequently than in the past, and are pursuing their* [Flower Wars?] *with much diligence.*

Word has come that one of the villages to the east of the River at which we traded has much sickness there now, so we will not stop there on the way back.

Meanwhile, much care. Allah preserve us, and I hope I shall ride your fine horse again soon.

Yours in business,
el Hama

I thanked the runner. He wasn't supposed to wait for an answer (the letter, he said, came from six days upriver from his village). I gave him one of my pipes, the best one I had made, with a catfish swallowing a frog. He thanked me

> "But who knows the fate of his bones, or how often he is
> to be buried? who hath the oracle of his ashes, or
> whither they are to be scattered?"
> — Browne, *Urn Burial*

and trotted away.

"Let's go talk to Sun Man," I said.

"He's getting ready for the Black Drink Ceremony," said Took. "He has to start fasting at sundown."

We walked between the huts and mounds to the plaza.

"By the way," said Took-His-Time. "Everybody's been asking if you're going to take part in the ceremony."

I stopped and looked at him. "That would mean they consider me to be one of the warriors, wouldn't it?"

"Nobody else brought such fine heads back from the Flower War," said Took, shaking his head in sad recollection of my wasteful act at the creek.

"What happens in the ceremony?" I asked.

"Well, the usual stuff first. Prayers to the harvest and the Woodpecker. Then all the warriors drink the Black Drink, and you shit and vomit for two or three days."

"Sounds wonderful."

"Cleans out impure thoughts. Makes for a great harvest. I was sick for a week last year, but we sure ate good the early part of last winter, didn't we?"

"Why me?"

"Well, Hamboon Bokulla and his gang are all implying that you like to have all kinds of warrior fun without any of the responsibility."

"Barfing is a responsibility?"

"In this case," said Took, "yes."

"Well, okay," I said.

"Okay," said Took. "No breakfast tomorrow, and you'll be sorry if you eat a big supper tonight."

We walked a little farther.

"Next thing you know," I said, "everybody'll be wanting me to get my dong whacked."

"Well," said Took, "there's been some talk ..."

"Count me out."

We went to Sun Man and told him what the note from the traders said.

———

We were all sitting in a big circle saying prayers. My mind was in neutral. Somehow I'd gotten seated between

Moe and Dreaming Killer. They were really into it, rocking, chanting. Sun Man, over at the top of the circle, was off in some other world, he was praying so hard and fast.

They were mostly thanking the Woodpecker and the harvest, and then two priests brought out this big boiling vat of something. It looked like crude oil and smelled like hot aniline dye. They dipped in three big bowls, holding two, and gave one to Sun Man. He stood up with the bowl.

"Great Woodpecker," he said. "Great Harvest Woman. With this drink we cleanse ourselves of impurities, and our minds of bad thoughts. We will all think of a great harvest. Let no one here be unworthy. Let anyone with unclean thoughts about the crops be struck dead as he takes his drink. Great Harvest Woman, Great Woodpecker, hear us!"

Then he drank two great big swallows.

They passed the other two bowls around, each man taking a drink, their faces screwed up in disgust and agony as their throats worked.

Took had told me it was considered polite to sit in the circle at least until the bowls made it all the way around, no matter *what* your stomach and guts did. I was halfway around the ring, so wouldn't have it as bad as those next to Sun Man. Took had already drunk his, and was stolidly saying something to his neighbors.

Hamboon Bokulla, the Dreaming Killer, swallowed his, some of the oily black drops, like thin tar, spilling onto the tattoos on his shoulders.

He put the bowl down and reached his hand toward his leather pouch.

Moe said something to me, joking about one of the priests, who was definitely in distress.

Dreaming Killer touched the bowl to my arm. I turned, took it from his hands. He watched me disinterestedly.

I held my breath, brought the bowl with its inklike brew to my lips, took a chug.

It was like ink and oil and lighter fluid. I wanted to gag but swallowed anyway. My throat and mouth, thank god, went numb like I'd swallowed novocaine. Anything was better than tasting it.

Then everybody was getting up from the circle and coming toward me. That wasn't right.

I was standing up. The bowl turned over and over, then bounced high from the ground, a long slow black line behind it in the air. The world was turning sideways and so was I, slowly. The world was faces then chests then legs then the dirt. I felt my arms hit a long time after my head.

They turned me over. I saw blue sky turning gray at the edges.

"You see," said Dreaming Killer, slowly, each word forming in my brain, "he was evil. He would have killed the harvest." Dreaming Killer was above me, finger pointing down.

"No," said Took. Dreaming Killer swam away, Took paddled into view, grayer and smaller, then my view swam away.

———

There was crying. There were hands touching me.

———

There were hands touching me. There was crying. I could say nothing. I could see nothing. I could not breathe.

———

I smelled cedar. I tried to move. There was wailing. I couldn't move. The first basketfuls of dirt were poured.

No I said.

Dirt came down.

No I said.

Dirt came down.

Dirt came down.

———

I heard fire. I heard running. I heard screams. I heard nothing.

the box

13

DA FORM 1   1400 Z   13 APR 2003

COMP _147_   TOE _148_

PRES FOR DUTY: _56_
KIA   _49_

KLD   8

MIA   30

MLD   1
WOUNDED, HOSP   3

TOTAL: _147_

FOR: S.SPAULDING   BY: ATWATER, WILLEY

COL, INF   CPT, ARMOR

COMMANDING   ADJUTANT

AFP 907-11M-996

DA FORM 1   2206 Z 15 APRIL 2003

COMP __147__   TOE __148__

PRES FOR DUTY: 49

   KIA   61

   KLD   8

   MIA   13

   MLD   2

   WOUNDED, HOSP.   11

   AWOL   **TOTAL:** 1

                  147

FOR: ROBERT PUTNAM   BY: M. SMITH

MAJOR, AGC   CWO1

COMMANDING   ASST ADJUTANT

AFP 907-11M-996

"That's all we know," said Jameson to Captain Thompson. Thompson was tall, thin, with a small clipped mustache. He wore his dress uniform, and his issue raincoat dripped onto sorting tent ground cover.

"The Navy and the Department of the Treasury searches have all been just like ours," he said. "A few of the names match, but everything else is wrong, the ranks, dates of birth. May I see the things now?"

"Certainly," said Jameson. He opened the oiled rag on the table. "Use these tongs. Here's the magnifying glass."

It was quiet in the tent except for the constant spatter of rain on the tent roof.

"Do you know what these are?" asked Thompson.

"Pieces of metal with names on them."

"No, I mean, the tags themselves. Dog tags. They're like the ones the French and British used in the Great War. There's a move afoot to get us to adopt them in times of war. They wore them around their necks. When a body is found, the finder is supposed to put the tags between the incisors of the dead person, and to wedge them in with their rifle butts.

"Wonderful," said Bessie.

"Some bodies lie on the battlefields for months, or years. You'd know that metal wedged in the teeth would be about the last thing to disappear. Where are the inscriptions?"

B

E

S

S

I

E

11

"Hold them at a slant. They're pretty well obliterated by rust."

"Got it. Your eyes are a lot better than mine. You got seventy-five inscriptions off these?"

"There are eighty-two of the tags," said Bessie.

Thompson read: Putnam, Robert NMI RAO 431-31-1616 DOB 06-01-73 Catholic.

"No middle initial. Officer rank. The numbers aren't right. They're not ours. We use seven digits. The dates of birth are what's really throwing us. Most of these were from the '70s and '80s. We've never used identification tags like these. I went through all the personnel orders on the train, all the way back, trying to find anywhere or any time these could have been issued. Nothing, nowhere. And of course the latter parts of the century before last are out of the question."

"So you can't explain it any better than we can?"

"I don't even know what I'm looking for. How exactly were these found?"

Jameson sighed. "Bessie'll take you down there in a few minutes, as soon as we find you some high rubber boots. Kincaid's still down there with Perch and the photographers.

"There's a conical mound atop a platform mound. That's unusual. Connected to the bottom of the platform mound is another mound, filled with the skeletons of horses which seem to have been shot to death.

"The bottom platform mound is filled with headless skeletons. There are probably as many skeletons as there are tags; maybe more. They're lying feet outward, and fill up the whole mound. It is, we decided, what's usually called a trophy mound."

"That usually indicates a great victory of some kind," said Bessie. "What usually happened was that when a leader suffered a great victory, he had all his enemies killed, beheaded and buried in one place. This is one of the largest of those ever found."

"What happened to the heads?"

"The chief usually kept them as trophies as long as he lived."

"Pretty outré."

"In this case," said Jameson, "they buried their great leader on top of his own trophy mound."

"You're sure it's the same Indian?"

Bessie looked at Jameson. "Pretty sure. One, the connection between the mound full of horses and the one with the human skeletons. On top of the one with the skeletons, they built another mound, using different soil. The bottom of that upper mound was paved with human skulls, lots of them. Atop them was a log tomb, with an upright burial. They usually reserved that for their royalty. The burial was filled with grave goods. Some of them were anomalous."

"What?"

"They shouldn't have been there. Anyway, around the upright skeleton was a necklace, with these identification tags on the necklace."

"That makes you sure it was him?"

"Nothing makes us sure of anything," said Jameson. "Remember I told you the horses had been shot?"

"Yes."

"Well, the chief buried in the upright position had a gunshot wound in the elbow. The wound had healed badly. It looks as if the person lived another twenty years after the injury. Why else would they bury you with a bunch of heads, on top of a mound of headless skeletons, unless those heads belonged to you?"

"Let me get this right. Those people were killed with firearms, and the ID tags give their birth dates as in the 'seventies and 'eighties? I thought all the Indians were run out by Andy Jackson in the 1830s?"

"That's what we're trying to find out, Captain. Either we're dealing with a remarkable hoax, and if we are, why don't the numbers match like you say, or else we're left with the only conclusion we have — that the people who built these mounds died out around the year 1500 A.D."

"Jesus Christ on a crutch!" said Thompson.

I woke to the smell of dirt and fire and wood.

At first I couldn't move. Then I remembered the black drink, and the tomb and my helplessness.

Slowly I began to move my arms and legs. I couldn't make a sound; my throat wouldn't work. I pushed, felt wood. I was weak, my arms were like rags, and my chest felt hollow.

I heard something outside, moaning or wailing. I got my shoulder up against an overhead log and pushed. It gave a little, bark scraping into my skin. They'd put one of the damn copper gorgets on my chest; it was digging into my flesh. I jerked at it and nearly cut my throat on the necklace that held it in place.

There was a club and hatchet in there with me, and god knows what else. I moved them out of the way.

I pushed again. Dirt ran down into my face in the darkness. I got a hand in the space, heaved up. A tiny piece of daylight appeared. I heaved at the log, got a fist-sized clod in the left eye. Blind, I forced my arm up, clawed, sat up.

I wiped more dirt into my eyes, trying to clear them. I jerked another log away.

The mound was less than a meter high around me, only the start of one.

When I could see, I saw that the walls of the stockade were charred and black to the east. There were only five or ten houses left where once there had been fifty. Smoke hung over the village. Warriors stood on the walls, heavily armed.

There were twenty or thirty people standing ten meters away, some with their mouths open, looking at me.

**L
E
A
K
E**

13

"To be gnawed out of our graves, to have our souls made drinking bowls, and our bones turned into pipes, to delight and sport our enemies, are tragical abominations, escaped in burning burials."
— Browne, *Urn Burial*

I scraped both my legs on the log bark, reached back in and pulled out the club and my javelin. I had to move broken pots and pipes around to do it.

My stomach was an empty pit. One of the men had a ripe may-pop in his hand.

"Food," I said, my voice as caked with dirt as I was.

He handed the may-pop to me. I swallowed it in two bites. A boy handed me some plums. I ate them, seeds and all. I drank from someone's waterskin.

Sun Man hurried up with two or three of his close followers, all armed.

"How long have I been in there?" I asked.

He studied me a moment. "Three days," he said. He reached out and touched me. "It's good to have you back," he said.

Two of the Buzzard Cult guys, all tattoos in the morning light, stood halfway across the plaza from us. They pointed at me, let out whoops, ran back toward the huts to the north.

The village was half gone with fire, torn buildings, over-turned goods. In front of the temple mound, bodies were laid out in neat rows, three of them. Two men were cutting up house logs nearby. Others were pulling arrows and spears out of the ground and houses where they had stuck.

"What happened?" I asked the people. Someone handed me dried fish.

"We were burying you," said Sun Man. "Many were still feeling the effects of the Black Drink. The Huastecas attacked us at evening. We have been fighting them for two days. They have gone now. They have killed many, took many prisoners. They got inside the walls twice."

"They just attacked, with no warning?"

"None at all. Their honor is gone. Their god has driven them crazy."

Sunflower was running across the plaza her arms out to me, crying. She ran into me. I grabbed her and she kissed me. Sun Man looked away.

"Took was captured," she said. "They have taken him away. I thought I had lost both of you." She buried her head. "I just heard you had come back to life."

I was weak and had a moment of vertigo. I needed a lot more food, water, a bath.

"How long have they been gone?"

"The last of them left before dawn. They probably left with the prisoners last night. There was not much we could do to stop them," said Sun Man. He looked very tired and old. Half his village was dead or taken prisoner.

"Is my horse still alive?"

"The Big Dog? Yes."

"Could you have someone get me food? I'll be at the temple in a few minutes."

I led Sunflower toward the hut. It was still standing, though the thatching was burned. Over at the north end of the village the Buzzard Cult people were starting one of their dances.

"They sound happy," I said. I went to my skins, reached under them and took out my waterproof bag. I pulled out the carbine, put it together, loaded up all my extra magazines and put the bandoliers together.

"You're going after them?" asked Sunflower.

"Yes."

"Then I'm going to lose you both again," she said.

"I hope not. I'll bring him back. I'll bring them all back."

"No, you can't," she said. "You are one man. There are more of them than there ever will be of us."

"I'll do what I can," I said. I picked up my gear.

I hugged her to my dirty body. She kissed me. "I'll bring him back. Stay here. Take care of everybody."

I went back past the plaza and out to the River. I put my things down, jumped in, washed the dirt and grit of the tomb off me.

Several dozen people were watching me as I came back in the gate with my fatigues on. I went over to the pen and saddled my horse and brought him around to the front of the temple mound.

I passed the rows of bodies. Curly and Larry were there, their tattoos as bright in death as they had been in life. Larry's head was turned wrong. Curly had two or three holes in him.

Dreaming Killer lay not too far away.

I handed the reins to one of the priests. He didn't like it, but he held them. The horse was nervous.

"What about Moe?" I asked Sun Man, using his real name.

"Captured. I think he was knocked out when they got him. They wanted a lot of prisoners." A woman came up and handed me enough food for four days.

"It is four days' hard march due west," said Sun Man. "It is a big city. They will kill you before you can get to the gates."

I turned and went up the stairs toward the temple, which had been rebuilt after the fire during the storm last fall. A priest made to stop me. Sun Man held up his hand. He waved to the priests at the top. They stepped aside.

As I walked up I heard the sounds of axes chopping the logs for tombs. People scraped dirt loose from the far edge of the plaza, preparatory to the funeral rites and the start of a new mound. The village around me which had once been beautiful in its way was now charred and half in waste.

I went into the darkness of the temple. I went into the inner sanctum. I picked up the Woodpecker God costume from its box and stuffed it into my pack. Then I put the head-piece with its bright scalp and gleaming bill under my arm.

I came back out to the top of the platform. The air was blue, the sun bright to the east. It was a beautiful morning up above.

Someone yelled when they saw what I had. The high priest dropped to the ground like a stone and lay still. The priests on the temple steps didn't move.

I went down the steps to my horse.

I swung up into the saddle and tied the pack to the saddle horn.

The people all bowed except for Sun Man.

I turned the horse and rode out across the plaza, and out the west gate. It slammed shut behind us.

I put our shadow in front of us.

The motorcycles and the gleaming white cars pulled up onto the bluff. There was a break between storms. The waters of the bayou lapped against the coffer dam and its sandbags; eating at it.

Men in black suits with bulges under their arms jumped off the cars, eyed people with lizard-like gazes, moved some of the crowd back.

Perch and Kincaid went to the middle car of the five. A man in a white suit and hat lounged in the back of the car. He sat up on the folded convertible top, looking at the tents, the dam, the mounds, the bayou.

Bessie watched from her tent. She was tired; she wanted to sleep for weeks. She saw Kincaid and Perch point to the bayou waters, the mounds, the dam. They indicated the workers filling the sandbags, the mired tractor, the tarps and tents over the mounds.

Then they talked like she had never seen them do before; their hands shaped mounds, crowns, royalty, lost heritages, millennia, mysteries. They talked for ten full minutes.

Bessie came from her tent and walked to the knot of men. One of the bodyguards nodded to her. She walked up within a few feet of Kincaid as he finished his plea.

The man in the white suit pulled a long cigar from his left coat pocket, pulled off the cellophane but left the band on. He snipped off the end of the cigar with a penknife the size of a fingernail. He looked down at the mound, over at the bayou.

B
E
S
S
I
E

12

He lit the cigar.

"Bodeaux?" he said around it.

"Yo, Kingfish!"

"Call the highway department. Give these people what they want."

"Yes, Kingfish."

Then the man in the white suit winked at Bessie. She blushed.

Men jumped on running boards up and down the line. Sirens started up. The motorcycles wheeled ahead. The cars bounced back to the road, the man in the white suit puffing on his cigar.

As the convertible turned its wire-spoked wheels out onto the road toward Baton Rouge, he flicked his cigar out onto the highway and put his hands behind his head.

I rode west, and the trail wasn't hard to follow. They must have walked eight abreast when they left the siege. It looked like someone had driven herds of cattle through the grass where they left the trail.

I was weak as a kitten. The jolting of the horse didn't help. I kept it at a steady trot, stopping to rest and water it every two hours or so.

When it got too dark to see, I stopped for the night, hobbled the horse and fell into an exhausted sleep, a free-lunch counter for mosquitoes.

**L
E
A
K
E
14**

I rode west, and the trail wasn't hard to follow. They must have walked eight abreast when they left the siege. It looked like someone had driven herds of cattle through the grass where they left the trail.

I was weak as a kitten. The jolting of the horse didn't help. I kept it at a steady trot, stopping to rest and water it every two hours or so.

When it got too dark to see, I stopped for the night, hobbled the horse and fell into an exhausted sleep, a free-lunch counter for mosquitoes.

Dawn came up like thunder, and the noise caused me to have a splitting headache. I ate half the food I had with me for the whole trip, got some dirty water for my canteen, and rode again.

Soon I left the last of the country I knew. We went through flat land with high grass, water, pines. A rice grower's dream, if there had been any rice in this part of the world yet.

I was fevered and aching, but in pretty good shape for a guy who'd been given up for dead and been buried for three days.

I had to catch up to the Huastecas. Maybe they'd lost their minds, like Sun Man said after the battle. They never

---

"Dead folks are past fooling."
— Thomas Fuller

attacked villages, except those of their own which were in constant revolt against them. They'd never come this far east. They had never fought to the death before that battle we'd had with them last moon.

What the hell. Is everything going to fall apart just when I show up? Maybe Dreaming Killer was right; maybe the Death Cult is on the right track. Maybe Death is becoming the next big thing in this world, after centuries of status quo.

I think of Took, Moe, the others. Headed for the cannibal pot, or whatever the Huastecas use. I kick the horse into a faster trot.

Night again, though I ride blind until long after I should. The horse feels the way. It's still like a two-lane highway through the grass. I stop when the grass changes to a packed-earth trail.

Morning. Calm. Outside the grove of trees in which we spent the night, the path goes straight as a bullet to the west. The land that way is flatter. A storehouse squats across the pathway. Somebody leans on a spear.

Their lands start here, then. I can't be more than thirty kilometers from their regional capital. Only a few hours behind them. They should have reached the city last night. I doubt they let the captives slow them once they got this far.

So this is it: man vs. society gone mad in a world he did not make. I ready my pistol and carbine while the horse grazes. I put on my helmet, and over that, and my back and shoulders, I drape the Woodpecker God costume.

Its giant beak hangs over my forehead. I tie the straps around my neck. I mount the horse, gentle it down, watch the stone house two hundred meters away. I hang my three grenades on the carbine sling.

A naked guy leaves the stone house at a hot trot, toward the west. A messenger, and what he has to say is all quiet on the Eastern Front. I wait until he's out of sight.

Then I turn the horse out onto the pathway and ride for the blockhouse.

The guy leaning on his spear comes up, looks at me, puzzlement on his face. Then he starts to yell, and guys come out like bees around a bear, spears up, sleepy-faced. Their waking-up faces change to Os, all mouth and eyes. While they stare, I ride right over them.

A spear comes past, already falling. I'm gone.

About a kilometer and a half past them, I see the runner ahead, still in his casual lope. He hears the hoofbeats, he turns his head, he gives a little jump, and when he comes down he turns into a copper streak.

The distance between us actually widens a moment. This guy is fast. Then the horse's hooves eat up ground. Ahead of the runner to the right of the path is a small stone shelter of some sort, maybe for travelers caught out in the rain.

We both close on it. I've got my club, and I raise it. He's looking back over his shoulder at me; he moves ahead again; I lean over to hit him as we draw even.

There is a dull crash and he disappears as the edge of the rock house whizzes past. Like a left fielder after a line foul, he's watching me and not the road, and he ran into the wall, face first.

I turn and watch him bounce once, sideways out into the pathway. I put up the club and watch my riding.

———

It's like I'm a pain in a body, and the runners are nerve impulses trying to tell the body that something's wrong. Only I'm moving faster than they are. My intention is to give the Huastecas a toothache all the way down to their insteps.

I pass more blockhouses, and other houses, too. I meet some runners. Some of the guards actually get off a spear or arrow before I go by.

The closest brush comes when I overtake one of the casual runners about half a kilometer before a blockhouse. There are cultivated fields all around now, but no one seems to be working them. A holiday? Of course.

Come see the gods eat the mound-builders. Have a bite while you're at it.

I'm thinking all this while the messenger ahead of me is in the low-running position. He looks like a cartoon, all arms, pumping legs, strobing bare feet. And he's still got lungs enough to yell so they can hear him at the guard-house.

There are four or five of them, they have lots of warning, they are awake. One of them's giving orders, they're fanning out, bracing their spears in the roadway, which is now four meters wide and occasionally paved. The guy giving orders is scared but grim.

The runner ahead of me gives one last burst and heads off into the field, trampling corn, duty forgotten.

I kick the horse and head for the waiting guards.

What they tell you to do with an arrow that's not in a vital spot is to push it through until the head pro-trudes, break off the shaft, and pull it back out the entry hole.

On horseback, that's not as easy as it sounds. The arrow was in the meat of my left arm. It already had an exit hole. I spurred the horse, got a kilometer past the guard house, then reined in.

I pushed the head the rest of the way out, screaming all the time. It felt like the world's worst zit pain all the way through my body. The arm went numb. I took out my bayonet, cut the arrowhead off, then tried to pull the shaft back out.

There was no way I could do it. I closed my eyes and yanked. The shaft came out of my arm; I came out of the saddle.

I held on somehow.

Behind me, they'd started a fire. Daring and resource-ful guards were getting word to the city. The King of the Huastecas would probably reward them with my head when they caught me.

I slapped a local anesthetic and an astringent on the hole, tied a dressing on the arm with the other hand, and turned the horse off across the fields, paralleling the roadway.

The city was like a white Oz. The suburbs, cornfields, sunflower stalks, old pumpkin vines, and small adobe huts had blocked my view long enough. When I came to a cleared plaza in one of the hamlets and saw the city, I thought I was on another planet.

It had a wall around it, but not a very high one. There was a river to discourage attack. What showed over the walls were gleaming brown and white buildings three and four stories tall. The tops of flat pyramids rose above those. There was some hullabaloo going on at the central one. That was my target.

The causeway over the river to my right was solid spears, shields, and head-dresses. The one to my left (the arm with the quickly returning pains) was sparsely defended, though the guys there were ready and waiting, too.

I headed into the river between the two bridges. The lathered horse plunged in. The water wasn't deep; I don't think the horse swam for more than a few seconds before it found bottom again, came up, plunged ahead. The bridge on the right emptied as the guards all ran back inside the city to cut me off.

From inside the city came the muffled sound of horns and drums.

The horse found gravel and bucked ahead. The guards on the left got ready. Arrows flew by me from the wall left and above.

We tore across the small beach. The suburbs and fields lay to the left, the city wall to my right shoulder. The guards on the causeway milled around, some heading back into the city, some running to the beach end of the bridge.

I kicked the horse and we went up, hanging in the air, shuddering, to the roadway toward the gate. Spears went by; one slid along the horse's neck and ricocheted back into the water.

We were up then, inside the gate, riding down two bowmen who tried to stop us.

Before we got here, it had seemed like the whole city was waiting for us, but as we went farther, I realized we were only some minor administrative inconvenience to the populace at large.

The streets themselves were deserted; the horse's hooves echoed off the empty houses. There were yells, and horns blowing behind me, other sounds from a side street. In the main plaza were the noises of muffled drumbeats and a ceremonial horn.

It was high noon.

Not even *Ben-Hur* made me ready for the scene in front of me. I slowed the horse to a trot. I came out of the narrow gate street into an open concourse beyond which lay the plaza.

In the center of the city, looming over it, the great white pyramid took a bite out of the blue sky. At its top, two fires in front of the temple poured smoke into the air.

Along the steps all the way up were armed guards.

At its base were other guards, and Took's people and other mound-builders, lined up in single file. The Huastecas, thousands and thousands of them, watched from the plaza, a gaudy smudge of headdresses, red and purple, jaguar skins, black hair, gold, copper, parrots, and obsidian, row on row on row.

Some of Took's people were strung in a line up the pyramid. At the top five priests waited. A mound-builder reached the top step as I reined in. Four of the priests grabbed him, pulled him backwards, chest up, over a rounded stone. The fifth priest, covered with something that looked like flapping gray rags, lifted a big black knife.

He brought it down. Blood went everywhere. He hacked and pulled. Another lump of blood flew into the air. The priest pushed his hand in the chest, hacked with the knife again. Something slid across the mound-builder's leg, onto the slab top. The priest reached down, picked it up. Blood dripped from it; it slipped through his fingers onto the victim's body.

The priest grabbed it again, held it up, then threw it into the leftward of the two fires.

The crowd yelled as the heart went into the flames: "Huitzilipochtli!"

The other four priests pushed the body to the left, over the pyramid steps, where the guards rolled it down the sides.

The festivities had just started. One body had already reached the bottom, two others were partway down. Huastecas wearing nothing but breechcloths picked up the first one and took it off behind a screen, stage right.

The line of Took's people and other strangers stretched across the plaza and back up into a building. The crowd was going to be very tired by the time the show was over. The priest and the rounded rock were already covered with blood.

There was a commotion and horns behind me as the gate guards got closer. Some of the crowd near me turned and saw:

The Woodpecker God of Took's people astride a huge dog on the road at the edge of their plaza.

I pulled the carbine from its boot and opened the action a little to break the partial vacuum and let river water trickle out of the barrel. The crowd near me drew back, confused, yelling.

The running feet behind me got closer.

The next victim had reached the top of the pyramid. Eager hands reached for him.

The head priest lifted his knife as the mound-builder went across the slab.

I blew the top of the priest's head off. I saw the other priests' reactions just as the sound of reached them. Why is our boss exploding his head and flying into the temple wall?

He slid down the alabaster wall, hair sticking to its surface.

The other priests turned toward the gunshot. I shot away the two holding the left arm and right leg. The other two let go.

There was pandemonium. The whole crowd in the plaza came to its feet. Took's people turned and saw me, then pointed and yelled.

I kicked the horse and headed for the pyramid. The crowd parted like the Red Sea, a moving wall of mouths, eyes, screams to either side.

I fired into them a few times for effect, then started on the guards on the pyramid steps.

Took's people were the first to come loose from the crowd. Something snapped in them; they turned and jumped everybody near them who had a weapon.

The intended victims all up and down the pyramid squatted while I shot the guards around them. Then I was at the bottom of the steps and rode up them.

Guards leaned around from the other sides of the pyramid, threw spears or shot arrows, then ran.

Took's people surged around me as I rode upwards. Moe came bouncing down from farther up. He picked up a spear and turned to watch the plaza.

Took yelled from the mob below. I turned the horse sideways, saw him, and waved. The city was a swirling, kicking mass. Too many warriors were standing still at the back center of the plaza around a white-poled sunscreen.

That must be where they keep their *kahuna*.

I fired into it.

For a few seconds the guards stood grim-faced while I shot them, then they broke to right and left, leaving richly dressed guys crawling over dead bodies for cover. I shot into the most swazee-looking bunch.

Two or three guards jumped in front of one of them. I shot them, but the magazine ran dry before I got a clear shot at the guy in the middle.

I slammed another magazine in, switched to automatic, and sprayed the emptying plaza.

We were on the pyramid, and they were behind all the buildings. The roof of the one across the way, the tallest, was covered with archers.

"How do we get out of here?" I asked.

"How about the way you came in?" asked Moe.

I looked that way. It was full of the shadows of spears and shields.

"Pretty grim," I said. "What about over there?"

There were screams below us as arrows came in. Every minute we stayed up here, someone was going to be killed.

I was still on the horse, which barely had room to stand. The men and women near the bottom were pressing up against us, trying to get away from the plaza. I didn't blame them.

I felt a dull thud and an arrow vibrated from the Woodpecker God's bill. I broke part of it off.

"It all looks bad," said Took-His-Time, just below me. Another flock of arrows sailed in, causing a rush as everyone tried to get behind the few shields we had. Most of the people on the pyramid had only spears, clubs, or knives.

I meant to ask Took sometime what it was that had turned his people from a line of docile sacrifices into fighters who had killed a few dozen of their captors and taken their weapons.

It was getting hot on the pyramid. I was sure the Huastecas were planning to send us a cool rain of arrows.

"Choose some goddam way!" I said to Moe.

"The way you came," he said. "Once we get to the gate, every man for himself!" They passed the word around the steps.

"Follow me, then," I said. I turned the horse to start down the *teocalli*. I fired toward the street we headed for. The sides of a building exploded in rock dust. A Huasteca screamed, a sound I was beginning to like.

The first mound-builders came off the pyramid. The Huastecas ran out from all the other buildings in a rush, throwing spears, clubs, and axes. They stopped, and the archers on the buildings sent another flight of arrows into us. A lot of us went down, some screaming, some not.

Then the Huastecas renewed their charge.

Still on the steps, I swung in the saddle and blasted left and right.

The mound-builders and Huastecas collided. The Huastecas who'd been waiting in the gate street came running out into the open. I fired into them. They stopped, jumped around, ran away.

"Go! Go! Go!" I yelled down to our people in the plaza.

They ran toward the street, scared, fighting, yelling, screaming.

More Huastecas came from everywhere.

The horse hit the plaza running.

Three arrows grew out of its neck. It collapsed. I rolled to my feet, still shooting.

the box

14

Smith's Diary   April 15

Colonel Spaulding duffed out during the night.

Nobody saw him leave. There were no shots fired during the night and no commotion from the Indians like they always make then they capture one of us.

Major Putnam is in command. He's demoralized by Spaulding's desertion, more than by anything else that's happened to us so far.

Spaulding had been keeping in his bunker. I saw him once yesterday afternoon. He had his Book of Mormon opened before him. I noticed the pages were more tattered every time I'd seen it, which was a lot. Spaulding seemed weighed down with worry. We'd lost more than half the group since the flu went through the Indians and started the siege.

I'd come to report that Sergeant Croft caught an arrow in the foot a few minutes before. He had leaned out to refill a sandbag. The arrow had come from the woods and into his boot. We didn't bother to return fire.

We knew they had at least eleven of our weapons. They had used them only a few times. One of the CIA men thought it was because they couldn't. Three of our people were dead from bullet wounds, and several of the horses had been wounded before we got enough bunkers built to hold them. The Indians were saving the carbines for something big. Besides, the arrows worked just as well in this short-range siege.

"How is Croft?" asked Spaulding.

"He's all right, but it'll be weeks before he's ready for duty."

"Weeks!" said Spaulding. "Soon you and I'll be the only ones left on duty." He stared down at his book.

"Some of the men want to clear the woods back another fifty meters to each side."

"What are the chances of doing that without taking three or four more casualties?"

"Not very good. They're everywhere, more of them all the time."

"Lamanites," said Spaulding.

"Beg pardon?"

He pointed down to the book.

"Oh," I said.

"They'll all be here soon. All the nations. We'll have to kill them all. It's so stupid."

I didn't say anything.

"All right," he said, regaining his demeanor. *"Have them put down two random grenades per day to each perimeter quadrant. We might discourage some of the sniping, anyway. Could you have the supply chief come over? I'm sure we're going to have to eat the last of the horses soon."*

I left. Splevins the CIA man passed me, heading toward Spaulding's tent. He didn't look happy. I dodged and crouched my way between bunkers.

That was the last time I saw Spaulding.

I was in the command bunker when the supply chief came in to see the major this morning.

"Things are missing," he said to Putnam. *"Damndest things."*

"I didn't think you kept inventory since Christmas," said the major.

"Some things yes, some things no. We just ran a tally on Spaulding's orders yesterday. They weren't there today."

The major sighed. *"What did he take?"*

The supply chief had a clipboard. He read off the expected things first — ammo, lurp rations, grenades, two ponchos, survival kit. Then:

"Grid maps. In series. From here through Mississippi, Tennessee, Kentucky, West Virginia, Pennsylvania to western New York state. Like he knows exactly where he wants to go.

"Tin snips. Two three-ring clip binders. Thin tin plate we had for repairs Cold chisels. Flashlights. A small radio beacon assembly. Tack hammer."

"What the hell's he gonna do with that stuff?" asked Putnam.

The supply chief shrugged. I went over to Spaulding's footlocker. I opened it. Most of his things were there, personal and issue.

"Not even a note," said the major. "I already had a look. His Bible's gone, though."

"How should we list him on the morning report?" I asked.

"Missing in the line of duty," said Putnam.

"Very good, sir," I said, and left.

We fought them out of the city and into the hamlets. There were more and more of them and fewer of us. We hadn't been that many to begin with.

We straggled through one of the garden villages and out into its beanfields. The Huastecas were close behind; arrows and spears were coming through the beans like snakes.

I was down to two magazines with maybe ten loose rounds left in my pockets. The carbine was holding them back, but they weren't showing much of themselves anymore, either.

A whole flock of arrows came down on us. We could see more Huastecas coming out of the city.

The beak on the woodpecker costume caught an arrow. It was hot as hell inside all those feathers. A Huasteca stepped out from behind a scraggly bush to use his atl-atl. I shot him somewhere low.

Took had picked up three spears from the ones thrown at us.

"They're going to run us in shifts," said Moe, pointing to where a line of Huastecas on the road were doing warm-up exercises. "They're in for the long push."

"Great."

"Well, you farted off their god," said Took. "We'd do the same for them. They never made it to our temple."

The warriors on the road were stripping to their breechcloths, picking up their weapons.

"I'll hold them a while," I said, like in the movies.

"Shit you will," said Moe.

He watched them a moment. "First they'll get you, then they'll get the rest of us. We've got to keep running at least as long as we can."

L
E
A
K
E

15

"The certainty of death is attended
with uncertainties in time, manners, places."
— Browne, *Urn Burial*

Some of the mound-builders had already taken off toward home. Their paths through the beans looked like rabbit runs.

"I'll see you back at home," said Moe. He put both of Took's arms on his shoulders and hugged him, then did the same for me, avoiding the woodpecker bill. Then he was gone through the beanstalks.

Took drew in a deep breath. "Let's go!" he said.

———————

Fifteen kilometers later the sun dropped at our backs. My lungs were tearing out. Six months earlier I would already have been dead, half the distance we had covered. My feet had become automatons. I was taking little short steps, stumbling.

I turned occasionally. I had only fired off a few shots, when one of the Meshicas was especially stupid. I only missed a couple of times.

The Huastecas seemed to be in three waves. The runners were half a klick back. There was a larger body beyond that, then half the city, way back of them. That much we saw from a small rise we went over.

I could see a few of our people, too, even with us, in flashes between the shrubs and crops. The Huasteca runners were slowly closing a pincers on us. It was still two kilometers wide, but I could feel it.

If we kept running like this, we'd smash into a tree trunk and do their work for them. We slowed a little, trying to see what was ahead.

"How-long-will-they-keep-on?" I asked.

"'Til-they-catch-us," said Took.

An arrow bounced off a tree trunk, to keep us honest.

———————

Sometime in the night we slowed, but so did the Huastecas. They didn't want to lose anybody either, but every time we crossed open spaces they yelled and drew closer. I couldn't see shit, but they could.

We heard victory whoops off to the left as somebody slowed to a walk and they caught him. I couldn't tell if they were killing and eating him on the spot or were taking him back to the slab as a real high tone sacrifice. I didn't have the breath to ask Took.

I just knew that I couldn't go much farther. I would be walking soon, and they could get me. I'd shoot myself in the head and spoil their real fun, but they would have the rest. I'd have to give Took the woodpecker suit first; I'd told Sun Man I'd bring it back.

It was probably pretty ragged by now anyway. The bill was flopping and the sound it made rustling wasn't as muffled as it had been.

Took stopped and I almost ran into him.

"This-way-follow-me." He pointed left. We came to some twisted old trees, thick as three men, with long low branches.

"Up!" he said. We went up the first one. I followed Took to the end of a low limb. He stepped across to the interlaced limbs of a second squat giant, then a third. I couldn't see anything, I could only feel a half-meter-wide limb under my feet.

We reached a fourth tree, in the center of them. Took pushed me toward a smaller limb. We must have been six meters up.

I pulled myself up into a bunch, trying to slow my breathing. The limb swayed in the slight breeze. My throat and nose were raw. I felt like lead.

We heard the runners go through below us, tireless, steady, probably a fresh gang. A few minutes later the second wave came through, somewhere between a trot and a fast walk. They talked among themselves. They were a long time passing under us.

Then we waited. It seemed like an hour; it was probably only a few minutes.

These people were having a party. They were laughing, talking, whispering; they barely moved. One leaned his spear against the tree next to ours and took a whiz. I couldn't see much, but didn't look down when some of them came by with torches. The largest bunch of them were singing some kind of war chant. We heard their armor clink, the padding of different feet, the creak of wooden shields.

There were hundreds of them, and they took an eternity to pass by.

I could barely make Took out. He was holding his fingers to his lips. We waited some more. The wind swayed the limb, not a pleasant feeling. The sounds died away in the night. I could see the faint blot of the torches moving east.

I started to say something, but Took put his hands to his lips again.

I heard a stealthy sound below, and through the blackness I saw a Huasteca, stripped and covered with dark body paint, edging through the tree trunks below. He searched the woods, stopped, waited two or three minutes, continued on, pausing again a few dozen meters on.

After a very long time Took said, "Try to sleep. Tomorrow they'll be back with the dogs."

Tying the carbine around my chest, I went to sleep.

the box

15

DA FORM 1

2206 Z 15 APRIL 2003
AMENDED 1206Z 16-APR-03 CWS

COMP ___147___   TOE ___148___

PRES FOR DUTY: X̶4̶9̶ 41 CWS

KIA   X̶6̶4̶X̶ 69 CWS

KLD   8

MIA   X̶X̶X̶ 16 CWS

MLD   2

WOUNDED, HOSP.   X̶4̶4̶ 10 CWS

AWOL   **TOTAL:**   1

147

FOR: ROBERT PUTNAM   BY: M. SMITH

MAJOR, AGC   CWO1

COMMANDING   ASST ADJUTANT

AFP 907-11M-996

Smith's Diary   April 16

I am in charge.

Atwater was killed when they overran the work party. It was a stupid idea and I said so. Then Atwater got himself killed.

A couple of hours later they fired a grenade that landed on top of the command bunker.

Putnam was killed by a piece of wood the size of a little finger. It went in just below his ear. There was very little blood, but he was dead.

Thompson is out of it, and has been for weeks. That leaves me.

We are down to fewer than fifty people who can do any good. The CIA people want their own command, which is fine with me. They refuse to accept a warrant office as commander.

I've got Hennesey making a beacon box, so maybe we'll be found sometime. All the reports and diskettes go in, this diary too, if we have enough time. He's got an old ammo box, some shellac and pitch. We'll seal it all in with the beacon, and finish this thing out.

I didn't want it this way.

I jerked awake and nearly fell out of the tree. The sun was up.

The baying of the dogs was what woke us up. Took pointed east toward the rising sun. "Let's go. Be careful. They're ahead of us."

We shimmied down the tree, the dogs getting louder to the left. We moved right and toward the sun.

As we made the next trees, I saw a line of Huastecas off to the north, moving slowly.

I still had a magazine plus a few rounds in the carbine, and the loose ones. The damn woodpecker suit was a nuisance. My muscles were cramped. The dew was still on the grass as we pushed through. The costume was soaked. But I'd told Sun Man I'd bring it back.

My breath was already rasping in my throat, and the arrow wound from the day before was stiff and burning.

They hadn't been after us, just making long sweeps through the ground they'd already covered, looking for strays. We knew that before we'd gone two kilometers. We slowed, became a little more cautious. Took stopped, dug around on the ground, came up with some peanut-looking things from under a dead bull nettle. They tasted like wood pulp but I ate them anyway.

We found a deep pine woods, dark and dry, and pumped through that. The sun was a slanting whiteness through the trunks. We followed it even though it ran to the south. But they would have to be in here with us to see us.

> "Who knows whether the best of men be known? or whether there be not more remarkable persons forgot, than any that stand remembered in the known account of time?"
> — Browne, *Urn Burial*

LEAKE

16

Then we hit a bayou full of cypress knees and rotten trees, crossing it as quietly as we could with muck up to our knees. I didn't want to think about the smell coming up from the water and black mud. It wore us all out. We crawled out onto the first dry land we came to, panting. I was lost.

"We're doing fine," said Took-His-Time, panting. "We go east until we find the River, then north or south to home. They won't follow us closer than a day's march out."

"They attacked the whole damn village four days ago," I reminded.

"That's because they're sneaky bastards. We've got plenty of warning this time. Sun Man's madder than hell, probably got everybody east of the Mes-A-Sepa over on this side waiting for them to try it again." He started to sit up, then thought better of it. "It's the next few hours we have to worry about."

"Great. It's the next few hours I want to lie here," I said.

From far off came the barking of dogs.

We were up and running.

———

Nearly dusk. Anybody closer than a kilometer could hear us breathing. Like freight train sounds. We'd seen one bunch of Huastecas going back the other way, either off shift on the chase, or with prisoners, or accompanying some noble. I didn't have enough shots for all of them, so we kept going.

There were probably a couple thousand of them between us and home.

As soon as it got dark, we stopped up another tree. It was by itself but was the only tree big enough to hold us both. The limbs weren't wide. I didn't like it. "I'll listen first," said Took. "I'll wake you up after a while."

I closed my eyes. Next thing I knew, Took was shaking me. "Your turn," he said, and went to sleep.

I waited. I listened. I watched, although I couldn't even see the tree we were in. The wind was cool. I shivered. It seemed like an eternity up there. I had no idea of how much time passed. I tried counting, got up in the high thousands, forgot it. As soon as I started nodding, I woke Took up again.

"I'm half asleep," I said. It sounded like he was rubbing his eyes. I lay back as well as I could on the limb.

I jerked awake at the same instant Took grabbed my arm.

The dogs were coming.

We ran into the trees. I fell down. The dogs were louder, closer. The sun was coming up. We headed for more cypress swamps, ran through them. I grabbed a limb at the water's edge once. It *moved*. I didn't even look back as the snake fell into the water behind us.

Now we heard yelling to both sides, and a horn blowing. They were closing in on us.

Dry land, more water, then land again. We ran toward the dawn, pushed more to the north by the sound of the hunt.

"They're ... trying ... to ... make us circle," said Took. "This way." He headed toward the sounds to the southeast. "I'd ... rather meet men ... than dogs."

I didn't want to meet either.

We came up onto a treed knoll, and we met both.

The Huastecas came up from behind bushes, throwing spears with their atl-atls and sicking the dogs on us. The spears were supposed to stop us so the dogs could bite out our assholes.

There were twenty dogs, all sizes, shapes, from ones that looked like Dobermans crossed with giant rats down to Chihuahuas. All I saw were eyes and teeth.

I started shooting, and Took and I slammed our backs against the nearest big tree. I was on my last full magazine. Took had the spear in front of him; he got a big dog in the chest with it. I shot one or two. They came under my fire and something clamped onto my leg. I smashed at it with the butt of the carbine. It squealed and let go.

Arrows and spears grew out of the tree behind us. I shot the biggest two dogs. Then the magazine was empty.

The Huastecas jumped up and ran for us, spears out, calling off the dogs.

I pulled the pin out of a grenade, pushed Took down and threw it at the nearest Huasteca. I saw him smile and catch it as I hit the ground.

He was turned into a fine red mist by the explosion that tore up everything in the grove.

I slammed my last magazine with six rounds in it home, and stood.

One guy was still standing, holding what was left of his stomach with what was left of his hands, eyes blank. Dead Huastecas and dogs lay everywhere. Some wounded of both kinds twitched.

Dogs were barking, getting closer, from another direction.

"Let's go," I said. I looked at Took.

He looked back at me. Half a meter of spear shaft, broken by the explosion, stuck out from his chest just below the clavicle.

"Oh, shit!" I eased him up, rolled him. The spear didn't go all the way through. There was no foam on the blood yet: not a sucking chest wound. I pulled the spear shaft slowly, twisting just a little as it grated on bone. I jerked open my first-aid packet from the web belt beneath the costume, slapped on antiseptic and stuffed the wound bandage into the edges of the hole.

"Hold that," I said. He raised his hand and pressed on the dressing. His eyes were coming back to normal.

The dogs were louder.

"Those guys," said Took, "must have had a canoe." Then he lapsed back into silence.

I jumped up, ran past the carnage. The Huasteca who was still standing walked out of the clearing, paying no attention to me or his wounds. He kept going.

Over where the next water started were three dugouts. I ran back to Took and helped him up. We made it to the canoe as the first of the dogs came past the dead men.

I was pushing out. Something hot and sharp stabbed into my calf. I screamed. Tiny growling sounds came up from my legs.

I grabbed my carbine, turning.

One of the Chihuahuas had me. Its teeth were like

needles. I tried to kick it away. Bigger dogs were coming. The thing was back, clamped on again. It wouldn't let go.

I used shot number one on the Chihuahua.

Number two on one of the big dogs.

Number three on a medium-sized one that bit the stern of the canoe and tried to drag it back to shore while I paddled.

Took was paddling with one hand, using the other to hold the bloody bandage.

We put out and made it a hundred meters into the bayou, dogs swimming in long V-wakes after us.

I used shot number four on the first Huasteca who got to the canoes. He fell dead. The rest of them stayed back in the brush until we got out of sight.

Otherwise it was a beautiful spring morning.

We were put up in an alligator run with the bushes closed behind us. It was past noon. I'd used the other dressing on Took's shoulder and hour ago. It was already soaked through. He lay in the bow of the dugout.

Occasionally we heard canoes go by, the paddles dipping in unison.

"I hate to tell you this," said Took, "but I don't think this bayou leads to the River. I was here once when I was a kid, before the traders, even. Unless you can carry this dugout on your shoulders, we're going to have to leave it a few hours' march from here."

"At least we can use it that far," I said.

Took looked at me for a long time. "What's keeping you going?" he asked.

"Well, I don't have a spear hole in my chest, for one thing. Your outlook will improve once you get a few days' rest and some food in you," I said, with a cheerfulness I didn't feel.

"They're going to get us," he said. "I have the feeling."

"Well, maybe. I've still got two grenades and two shots."

"One for you, one for me?" he asked.

"I won't like it any more than you will," I said.

"It'll be better than the slab."

"I meant to ask you about that." A bird squawked and flew away. We waited. Nothing happened.

"Your people seemed ready enough to die in the plaza. As soon as you saw me, you got your spunk back."

"When you're heading for the slab, in the chief city of your enemies, you might as well go as befits a man or a woman. When your god comes to rescue you, you fight."

"But it was just me in the woodpecker outfit, you knew that."

"I knew that, and you knew that," said Took. "But the Woodpecker God also knew that."

"And he approved?"

"I don't know whether he did or not, but he let you do it," said Took. Then he grimaced in pain.

"As soon as we get past the Huastecas, I'll give you something for the pain. It'll make you feel like you're flying. But if I give it to you now, you'll be unconscious for a day. I can carry you when we're past them, but not while they're around."

"We'll put out at nightfall," said Took-His-Time. "Go north, then east. When we get to the magnolias, we have to leave the canoe and go overland again. We should pass the last Meshicas before midnight."

He lay back in the boat, nodding, jerking awake, sleeping fitfully. The sun crawled like a bright slug across the sky.

Feet pounded on the bank once. The alligator came back, smelled us, and crashed back out of his run.

The sun dropped, then it was night.

———————

We pushed the canoe back out into the water and set off through the magnolia-scented night. "Home is that way," said Took, pointing. I couldn't see where he meant. "We'll join the path we followed to go to the Flower War last month, remember?"

"How far?"

"All night. Then home."

I turned and hugged him, careful of his shoulder. We

were using rags ripped from my shirt to stop the bleeding
now.

"We're going to make it," I said. "I can feel it."

"The night is long, Yaz," he said.

Right on cue an arrow whizzed by, then the darkness
was full of Huasteca whoops and hollers.

There were five or six of them and I got them with my
last fragmentation grenade. I didn't kill them all, just put
them out of commission. That woke up everybody, though.
The night filled with sounds after the echo of the explosion
died.

"Which way are we going?" I asked Took. I'd pushed
him down into the boat, and his shoulder was bleeding
again.

"That way." He pointed. The wind was blowing about
thirty degrees off that direction from our backs,
gusting.

"They'll be between us and home, won't they?"

"Yes."

"Then let's give them something to worry about
besides us. Stay down."

I took out my last grenade, a Wooly Pete. I waded to
shore, walked a few meters into the open space ahead. I
went to a position about twenty meters from where the
grass and underbrush were thickest. I pulled the pin and
threw the white phosphorus grenade that way, ran ten
meters and jumped behind a tree.

WP grenades are so heavy you can only throw them
twenty meters but they have a splash radius of thirty.

A firestorm bloomed on the night. I saw the bones of
my hand through the skin, it was so bright. I hoped
Huastecas for kilometers around had been looking right at
it; they'd be blind till morning.

The fire climbed up trees, over grass, along the ground
in a great red-orange and white wall. In no time it was a
hundred meters wide and growing, pushed by the
churning wind.

"Don't mess with the Woodpecker God," I said to
myself.

"Wow!" said Took, who was up and watching from the

canoe. The curtain of flames marched off toward the east, crowning trees, lapping at their trunks.

"Let's go home," I said.

———————

We found the trail at the same time the Huastecas found us.

They were to our left, the fire was to the right in a blazing arc a couple of kilometers long. The air was filled with escaping birds. The woods glinted with animal eyes, stopping and bounding away.

The Huastecas yelled. We saw them by the light of the flames. They saw us the same way. There were a dozen of them half a kilometer away.

"Can you breathe smoke?" I asked Took-His-Time.

"Maybe."

We ran for the fire, met deer coming out the other way. Before we even got close, smoke and hot air seared out lungs. An arrow flew by, its feathers bursting into flames as it ricocheted from a burning limb.

"They won't follow us in here," I said.

Took slowed, jumped some embers, slipped, fell into a smoking bush. The air was filled with cinders; burning leaves coaled into my cheeks as I bent over him.

Now there was froth on the blood from his wound. I took out the morphine injector, put it into his arm, and punched.

He went to sleep.

I pushed a few more strips of cloth into the wound, picked him up and put him over my shoulders in a fireman's carry. I walked with my burden through the ragged towers of flame that closed us in on every side.

Trees groaned and fell, spouting sparks, throwing fiery branches onto others. A smoking owl flew by. A raccoon ran into a hedge of fire. Smoke curled up from underfoot.

The world was orange, red, smoky. Feathers on the woodpecker costume began to singe and curl. I stepped on something live; I think it bit me. I staggered into cul-de-sacs of heat and fire, and back out again.

I walked until the bottom of the costume floated up around my waist.

I was surprised to find myself in water.

I carried Took for a long, long time. I was numb now, my lungs were burned, my legs had lost all feeling. I couldn't feel anything under them either. I slogged on through the water.

All the animals were there. Every bit of high ground was filled with eyes reflecting the fires, from the ground up to the tops of small trees.

Snakes and alligators swam by in the red-gold glare, bumping into my legs, backing off and going around. Something huge blotted out the light from the fire on one side, then was gone before I could see what it was.

The deeper I went into the swamp, the stranger it became. The glow was from both sides now. The fire had ringed or crossed the bayou somehow. Mist sprang up. I could no longer see the water, just a moving curtain two meters high in front of me. Overhead, the stars were obscured by roiling patches of smoke.

It got cold in spite of the fire. My teeth began to chatter. I was so tired I was trying to nod off as I walked. Things flitted in and out of my vision. I would jerk fully awake and they would be gone.

There was a third smudge of light ahead; when the mists cleared fro a few seconds I could see a blood-red moon with a bite out of it hanging in the east, like a half-closed rabbit's eye.

I was carrying Took now between cypress knees and stumps, thick and close-growing. The mists closed in again. I knew I was okay as long as I walked toward the glow that was the moonrise.

I entered shallower water. Took was an iron weight across my back. I moved him, shifting only a few centimeters. I was too tired to put him down and try again.

"Isn't he heavy?" asked a voice, long and low and booming through the mists.

"He's not heavy," I said, "he's my brother."

The moon was gone. There was a shadow before me on the water, black and long.

I looked up. A gigantic cypress tree stood before me. It had a limb halfway up that grew straight out from the trunk.

I looked down again, quick as I could. There was something on the limb, something half as big as the tree, something that blotted out the moonlight and threw the shadow over me and half the clearing.

"Who are you to wear the raiment of a god?" asked the voice. "You do not believe!"

My mouth wouldn't work.

"WHO ARE YOU?" it asked again. The long crested shadow before me turned, as if its great eye was scrutinizing me.

"I believe now," I said. "I believe in *this!*"

"You have burned my woods!" it said, its voice edging upward. "The lightning can burn my woods. Whole nations of men can burn my woods. One man *cannot* burn my forests!"

The shadow moved menacingly. I jumped backwards. Took whimpered.

"No more," I said. "Never again."

The shadow moved left and right as if surveying the damage all around.

"I didn't mean to burn your forests," I said. "I'm bringing Took-His-Time home. I'm bringing the raiment back to the temple. I'll never touch it again as long as I live."

"Easy for you to say," said the booming voice. It was quiet a moment.

"Tell them all," it began, and its voice had changed, "tell them all a great judgement has come upon them, and that I can't help them any more.

"All the gods are going tonight. We will not be back. Tell them they are on their own, tell them ..." And here the voice changed again, became a little less godlike, "tell them Hamboon Bokulla was right, he and the others. Tell them Death is God now; he is alive, he is walking. Tell them, Yazoo, that I wish them well."

The great shadow lifted from the water. The moon came back. The sound of flapping wings, huge, close, grew lower, farther away to the west, was gone.

I heard its cry from far off, once, twice, sounding like "Good god, good god."

"Good God!" I yelled. "Good God!"

The sun was coming up. The fire was dying all around. I pulled Took from my left shoulder to change him to the other.

He was dead.

They were losing the battle.

Even with the highway crews and their machinery, the water crept up the dam.

The state water people would neither close the gates upstream nor open those down. Rivers were out of their banks for miles, farms were being covered and lost. The Crimstead house across the way was swallowed up — the state police had come the day before to help them evacuate.

Crowds had come to watch since the governor had paid his visit. LaTouche was charging them a dime apiece to watch. State troopers had been sent to keep them up on the bluff, out of the mound sites.

Perch had caught a bad cold. They had made him go back to the Dixie Hotel. Their own work crews were reinforcing the dam. The highway crew was leaving; they were needed to save lives, keep bridges intact.

"Just two more days," said Jameson. "Maybe we can find out in two more days." He looked up at the rain. "We'll have both mounds down to the ground by then. It's too damn wet to do anything right!"

None of them, Thompson included, had had more than a few hours' sleep for the last two days.

Kincaid and Johnson had removed the conical mound, then started on the platform. All the grave goods were in two tents now. Broken pottery, pipes, weapons, the breastplate and head decoration beaten copper, unidentifiable rusted things, more cartridges, shells, beaten gold ornaments were in the sorting tent.

BESSIE

13

The second was full of skeletons, the first they'd exposed from the platform mound, one of the horses, the upright chief's skeleton. Some of the skulls, exhibiting exit wounds, were in there among them.

The weather had turned the others to powder as they were uncovered.

The cook tent now covered the platform mound. Kincaid's tent, and one other, were over the horse mound.

Water had begun to trickle in through the sandbags. Kincaid sent the work crews to fill more and stack them.

The crowd of onlookers squealed and moved back on the bluff. Their cars, trucks and wagons clogged the highway turnoff. Rumors ran through the crowd ten times a day — they'd found a mound filled with gold, with giants, with elephants, with a wagon made of silver. Washington brought the latest gossip from the crowd to them every hour or so.

"How that stuff starts, I don't know," said Bessie.

Thompson was studying a long piece of rust. "This could have been a sword," he said.

"Or a rifle," said Bessie.

Thompson looked at her. She flipped through her field notebook, making sure each specimen was catalogued by its proper grid mark. She put the book down on the camp table.

"Dammit! We don't know any more than we did the first day!" she said.

"You've got the chief, and the ID tags."

"That's not the answer. That's more question," she said. There were oohing noises outside. Then yells near the mound. She stood up. She opened the tentflap. The skies were gray and rainswept. Down near the horse mound, several of the diggers were running back from the dam. A small jet of water curved out from it.

"Pull the tents," yelled Kincaid nearby. "Get everybody up here!" He stepped in, wet as an otter, his eyes red-rimmed. He slung his wet raincoat off.

"It's all lost, " he said to Bessie. "We've got everything we're going to find down there. The dam's going. We'll lose a few horse bones, some skeletons, maybe more grave goods. But there's no answer down there. We'll have to piece one together from what we've got here."

"I've come to the same — " she began.

There were whoops and hollers down the bluff. Kincaid stepped into the rain, yelled. "Get those kids outta here! The dam's gonna go! Hey you! Troopers! Get — " He began to cough, great coughs that turned into ragged sobs.

Bessie held him while he cried.

"Jameson, I need a drink," said Kincaid after a moment. "People let their goddam kids down there. They want them killed, I guess. I'm going to have a big drink and watch the dam burst. Coming with me?" He and Jameson left.

In a minute, she heard "Potato Head Blues" crank up on the phonograph.

She turned. Thompson had his head turned at an odd angle. "What's wrong?" she asked.

He went to the table, turned her field book right side up.

"Oh, I see. It's the tents. For a minute, I thought you were drawing a defense perimeter."

Something went through Bessie like it had the night Bob Basket disappeared in the storm.

"What did you say?"

"I see now. Nothing."

"What did you *say*?"

"Your notebook. I looked at it upside down. It looked like a defense perimeter, a pentangle. Center command post, five bunkers around it. For defending ground like this. I see now it's the mound, and two of the tents on the bluff, and these three things marked 'shallow pits.'"

"If you were in one of those, and wanted to hide something, where would you put it?" she asked.

"You mean in combat? Under siege?"

"Yes."

He looked at the page a moment. "One of the bunkers. Under a bunker wall. They'd go by it on the way in. They'd search your command post with a fine tooth comb."

"Grab your shovel," said Bessie.

━━━━━━━━

They could hear the water up, higher than their heads. They were in the one shallow pit beyond the mounds inside the dam wall. The dam loomed like a frozen wave, its sandbagged top like bad teeth.

The crowd watched them expectantly. There were kids' footprints all around where they dug.

"Little hellions," said Bessie.

"Uh, I don't like that breach in the wall over there, Bessie," said Thompson. The small gurgle was now a steady dirty flow. Rain fell into their faces. The top of the bluff was a mushroom bed of umbrellas and sheets with faces under them.

"What are we looking for?"

"Anything," she said. "We won't find it. Give a yell when the wall gives way."

"Before then," he said.

They worked on in the rain. "Potato Head Blues" floated from the camp, made them work faster. The drainage pit the highway people dug was filling. Soon the water would rise and creep into the pit where they dug.

"How will we know when we find anything?"

"You've been digging through post mold for the last five minutes," she said. "Lots of it, more than for a wall."

There was a scream from the bluff. Some sandbags slid down the inside of the dam wall. Water sheeted in behind them.

"Bingo!" said Thompson. He put down his shovel. "Keep digging," said Bessie. He picked his shovel back up, dug in the wet earth.

There was a crash behind them.

They lived there for a year, Basket had said. *They raised crops.*

"Look out!" yelled a state trooper from above. They heard the dam tear.

They thanked the catfish and the crow, he had said.

Her shovel scraped something.

"Help me," she said.

Their shovels scraped. "Help me!" she said.

She found The Box.

They grabbed at it, lifted. It cracked. Water sloshed into their legs. They held the box together and ran. Water hit the backs of their knees.

"Kincaid," she yelled. "Help!"

The dam burst.

The trooper's face was all eyes and mouth. Bessie fell. Something pulled her by the feet, upside down, up the bluff face. She didn't let go of her hold on the box.

A million gallons of water smashed the bluff face below her head.

Upside down, she saw skeletons and horse bones flying around like tumbling dice.

There was a small sign, too, that said SEE ROCK CITY.

The village was quiet and there were no guards out.

Then I saw the buzzards, some flying low, some sitting still in the trees nearest the walls.

Then I heard a low chanting coming from inside.

I rearranged Took on my shoulders and walked in through the west gate.

The smell hit me then. Death.

A small group of people danced in the center of the plaza. The rest of the huts seemed empty, or places filled with the dead.

I went to the dancers.

**L
E
A
K
E

17**

They were Buzzard Cult people, and Moe was in there with them. They continued to dance in the bright sunlight as I walked up to them, still in the woodpecker skins.

Moe left the group and came to me.

"Where are the others?" I asked. "Did the Huastecas attacks again?"

"Those that are left are across the River," said Moe. "They have abandoned the village. They carried their gods with them," he said, pointing to the temple. The woodpecker effigies were gone.

"I wasn't the Huastecas," Moe continued. "Hamboon Bokulla was right. Look around you," he said, sweeping his arm over the still village. "Death came, a disease, while we were gone. We found the last of them. They sneezed and coughed up blood. Their skins burned to the touch and had turned purple with spots. They raved and they died yelling for water. It was not nice. You can look if you want. We only found the last few, and one old man who lived through it. The others are all east of the Mes-A-Sepa, starting over."

> "Some bones make best skeletons,
> some bodies quick and speediest ashes."
> — Browne, *Urn Burial*

"Are there any canoes left?"

"Take mine," said Moe. "I won't need it any more."

"What are you going to do?"

"We? We will dance up and down the River, bringing news of the coming of Lord Death to all who will listen. Eventually there will be many more of us, even on your side of the River. Death is here, Death like we have never seen. Perhaps it will take the Huastecas too, and they will join us in our dances. Perhaps we shall all die soon. It is the End Time. Will you join us in our dances?"

I thought of what the Woodpecker God had said, and looked at the dead village. I felt Took's weight on my back.

"No," I said. "Perhaps we will meet again. I have to give Took back to his people."

"A happy death to you, then," said Moe. He started to walk away, then turned. "Thank you for saving me from the slab so I could see the triumph of Lord Death." Then he rejoined the shuffling dancers — two steps left, half step, two steps right, his crying skull tattoos shining in the morning sun.

I found Moe's canoe at the landing, put Took-His-Time in the bow and paddled across the water, every muscle aching, fatigue hallucinations jumping at the corners of my eyesight. The River was a bright sheet of mud. More and more buzzards were circling in the skies, west of the River. Perhaps the dancing of Moe's people was keeping them out of the deserted village, maybe something else.

The people were easy to find. A few skin huts stood on a small bluff half a kilometer down and across the waters.

I put in to the landing where other canoes lay. Somebody blew a conch horn. I carried Took up the bluff across my arms. A small crowd gathered.

I saw familiar faces. Coming toward me in Sun Man's robes was his nephew on his sister's side. I looked past him to the far corner of the huts where a clearing had been made. In the center was a small mound covered with charcoal. Past it the three woodpecker effigies stood blank and silent.

I heard crying, and Sunflower came up to me, touching Took's body with her hands. I carried him toward the charcoaled mound, still warm from Sun Man's funeral. Sunflower helped me straighten the body. Others went to the hut and brought back a handful of Took's unfinished pipes.

We arranged them around his head and on his chest. Someone brought a torch. We put a few dried limbs and chips on him, and dragged some brush over to the mound.

Then I pulled off the woodpecker outfit, beak upward, and placed it on top of Took-His-Time, and was handed the torch.

"He told me to tell you," I said, and lit the costume which burst into flames, "that He is gone." I pushed brush onto the fire, then went to the woodpecker effigies. I pulled and pushed one and lay it across the flames. Then another and the other, straining and sweating under their weight.

Then we stood and watched the smoke and flames rise into the buzzard-dotted sky. Sunflower cried beside me. Sometime before the flames died down, six days and nights of fatigue crashed over me, and I slid down into bright blue dreams.

the box

16

Smith's Diary   April 17, 2003

This will be it.

The diary goes in the box with the official stuff and the beacon. I hope someone finds it.

It is quiet out there, and a starry night.

They are out there, more of them than we ever thought there could be. They seem to have been coming for days, from all directions, and now they are ready.

They mean to kill us all, or make slaves of us — whatever it is they do.

I can't blame them, but I don't want to die either, so far away from everything. We will kill each other tomorrow.

Hennesey is ready. God have mercy on us, and them too. We can't help being what we are. Neither can they.

We tried.

DA FORM 1   18 APRIL 2003 (AM)

COMP 147   TOE 148

PRES FOR DUTY:	34
KIA	85
KLDTY	9
MIA	16
MLDTY	2
AWOL	1

TOTAL: 147

FOR: B.F. JONES   XBYX   M. SMITH

ASST STA CHIEF   CWO1 RA

CIA   ACT COMM.
CIVILIAN CONTGT   US ARMY GP.

AFP 907-11M-996

The Box lay on the table in the humidity-controlled room in the University museum.

The team slowly opened it around the cracked place, removing the chipped shellac and pitch until they could get to the seams and pry them.

The wood came off in slips thin and pliable as paper.

It took hours to get it open.

Inside was rot and mâché. There were hard flat disks that could not be moved. They had become part of the box walls.

There was a book, its covers ghosts, its pages spiderwebs, but they could see words. There was a ream of paper solid as a butcher block. There was a small black box gone to sludge, with metal inside showing dimly through.

"It'll take months to dry the pages and separate them," said the curator.

"We've got nothing but time," said Bessie.

B
E
S
S
I
E

14

the box

17

On the side of the box, beneath the coat of pitch hardened to an amber-like material, and the cracked layer that had once been shellac, was a message in smeared grease pencil:

KILROY WAS HERE

and underneath, another hand had written

BUT NOT FOR MUCH LONGER

Light cold rain pattered against the top of the bluff. The wind was from the north. Cold gusts whipped Bessie's rubberized raincoat against her legs. The weather had changed. There would be sleet before nightfall, possibly snow by tomorrow night. The weather was as crazy as the rest of the year had been.

She looked down at the dark waters of the bayou. The top of the mounds was already under four feet of water — all the work of the summer obliterated as if it were a slate wiped clean. There was nothing left of the site but the specimens in the museum, her and Kincaid's notes, the Box. All the trenching and leveling, the work, the coffer dam against the rising flood was down there, known to catfish and gar.

There must have been a last stand and a final massacre. Just over there had been where the Box was buried. Right down there were the mounds where the old chief had had their bodies piled and the heads taken home. It was also where they brought him back when he died and buried him some years later, on top of the dead in their mounds, next to their horses.

Two cultures must have clashed there, neither able to understand the other, or help the other. A small drama in the scheme of things. Now traces of both were gone, relics of two doomed groups. One wiped out by their ancestors, the ancestors themselves then swept aside by the roll of time.

BESSIE

15

Bessie shivered for the future, for all futures. She leaned against Captain Thompson, who was lost in his own thoughts.

"None of it was fair," she said.

"Of course not." He watched the sleeted waters of the bayou.

"They should have let us find out more. They should have closed down the whole state. They should have let Baton Rouge drown. They..."

"You know all of it, don't you?" he asked.

"No! I want to find out *why* it happened. I want to *understand*!"

"They killed each other. They couldn't get along."

"No. The ones from the future, Up There. Why couldn't they have been wiser, kinder? Something? They came from a time when ..."

"I don't know. Why do people do anything?" Thompson threw his cigarette out in a spinning arc off the bluff. The twisting red dot winked out in the waters.

"A copy of the report's back at my hotel room. You can read it tomorrow," he said to her. "I wrote down just what happened, and what you found. I sent photostats of all the things we *could* copy. Kincaid will send a copy of your final papers. That's all I can do."

"Will it make any difference?"

"I don't think so," he said. "It'll be strange reading for some archivist. Somebody might want to do something with it, but what can they do? They can't change the past."

"But the future! That can be changed."

"I hope so. But we don't even know the terminology, half of it. People at the War Department will start asking about what some of the things are, and I'll try to tell them what I *think* they are. Then they'll ask you about all the Buck Rogers stuff. I'm sure *Amazing Stories* or *Weird Tales* will be interested, but that's about it. That's the kind of reaction I'll be getting."

"But proof. We've got it."

"Look," he said. He put his hands on her shoulders. "It's all very fine, what you have, for a museum, for what the average bloke thinks. But when you start waving it around in public, that's when you get in trouble. You know that. Look at that ... what, the ... elephant thing ..."

"Cincinnati tablet."

"That. That's been nothing but trouble, and still nobody's convinced. All you can do is try to prove this to your colleagues."

"And you?"

"I'm going to quietly insist to my superiors. That's all I can do. Any more, and they'll quit listening."

"Kincaid's going to deliver his paper when he finishes it."

"I wish him luck. There'll be cries of hoax before he's halfway through."

"I know."

They were silent. The sleet began to fall harder.

"We'd better go," said Thompson. "These roads are bad enough without this freak ice storm."

Bessie climbed into the Army truck beside him. He cranked it up and turned on the headlights. The truck faced the bayou. Through the sleet and rain she saw the waters of the bayou flat and black before them. This time next summer they would be another six feet higher. The whole landscape would be changed for hundreds of square miles around.

Thompson turned on the wipers. "There's a bottle of coffee back there; find it, will you please?" He turned the truck around. "I'm chilled through."

She rummaged behind the seat and found the warm jug. She looked out the rear window, saw the waters being lost in the darkness.

"They didn't understand," she said.

"No, I expect they didn't," said Captain Thompson.

He put the truck in low gear and bounced past a mudhole.

Things aren't normal, and they never will be again.

Every day Sunflower and I and a few others go and pile some more dirt on Took's mound.

Every day I work a little at the pipes Took-His-Time left in rough form, and finish them up a little more.

Every day brings new horrors to which we have grown numb.

Stories come from upriver on both sides: villages deserted, given over to the woods.

The Buzzard Cult people danced by one day last week, still across the River. We all watched. Their hands are joined, they do their shuffling steps for kilometers at a time. We hear they dance into dead villages, through their plazas, out the gates again.

When they danced back by again, earlier this week, there were fewer of them.

Our hunters who go back across the Mes-A-Sepa keep away from the towns and solitary huts, any place that had been settled by man.

The only good news to come across is that the Huastecas seem to be dying faster than we ever will, from some other disease, or with the same one with a whole new set of symptoms. Theirs sounds like mumps to me. They got it way down on the Gulf where their merchants had set up permanent trade with the Traders during last winter.

The Traders and Northmen are being hunted and killed wherever they are found. I hope some of them get away. The diseases are here; it's too late to stop them. Killing the messengers is futile. It probably makes the people feel better.

L
E
A
K
E

18

> "them bones, them bones gone walk aroun'
> them bones, them bones gone walk aroun'
> them bones, them bones gone walk aroun'
> nunc audite verbum dei"

On this side, the Buzzard Cult is growing, too, but slowly, quietly. They get together and dance, then they go home. Without the Woodpecker, there's not much else. The tattoo man is busier than ever. Weeping eyes are the next big craze, also hands and eyes, and rattlesnakes.

There is death and resignation all around.

Sunflower tries to keep busy and to keep me happy. I have to go out with the other guys now and hunt. It's late spring, and we're not sure if the crop we planted over here will make it. We're killing and drying meat as fast as we can. Maybe that mammoth will come back this winter, and if the pipe magic works, we'll all eat good.

I was carving on the pipe, trying to get the tusks just right, when they started yelling my name outside.

"Yaz! Yaz!" called the new Sun Man.

I came out with my spear.

The new Sun Man was already deeply tanned. He was carrying a small deer over his shoulder, something the old Sun Man would never have been seen doing. Everybody was out hunting and grubbing for roots.

Three guys who'd been across the River with him were there.

"Yaz," said one, pointing back over the water. "The place you came from. Remember? Something funny's going on there."

"What?"

"The air is weird. It moves. Next to the tree where you tied the white cloth, and laid the orange thing on the ground. We ran a rabbit through there, and it went away, right in front of us. We watched the air move for half an hour. Then the air started making hooting noises. We left in a hurry."

"Thanks," I said. "I'll take care of it."

I went back inside our skin hut.

"What's up?" asked Sunflower. She looked over her shoulder at me.

"Oh, guy-stuff." I rummaged around. "Sun Man wants me to take care of some business for him."

"Will you be gone long?" she asked.

"I don't know."

"Is it across the River?"

"Just a little way."

She looked at me darkly. "Do you need some food?"

"A little." I got some Army stuff I might need out of the bundle.

Sunflower gave me some food, leaned up and kissed me on the head. "Hurry back," she said.

I walked to the flap.

"Tell me if you're going forever," she said, very quietly.

"I don't think so," I said.

I kissed her. She looked away.

I went down to the River and picked out a canoe. There were lots not being used these days.

I had almost forgotten how the place looked, the bluff, the faraway bayou. It was noon the next day when I got there. I heard the hooting a long way off — a rising and falling klaxon sound, cycling about once every two minutes. It should keep the animals away, and bring in curious people.

Only there weren't any curious people within twenty kilometers any more. I doubt the Buzzard Cult people this side of the River would pay much attention. They'd probably think it was just one more manifestation of Lord Death. Maybe they would take notice, and build a shrine to it when they found it.

The air was shimmering. Somebody was still alive, Up There. They must have found a way to reconnect me. Good old Dr. Heidegger. Maybe his sons or grandsons or daughters. Or someone ten thousand years from now, who'd read his notes and duplicated his experiments as a curiosity.

I picked up a one kilo rock, took out my map-marking grease pen, wrote WHO ARE YOU? on it, stepped out where the front of the gate should be, and tossed it gently in.

Then I dived flat to the ground.

Nothing happened. The air kept shimmering, the sound rose and fell.

For an hour. Then the sound stopped. Chills ran up and down my spine.

A little more than an hour later, by my watch that still ran, the rock came back out. It rolled to within a meter of me. Beneath my message was the hastily scribbled HEIDEGGER. LEAKE?

I wrote ONE HOUR DELAY — ROCK COMING THROUGH. WHAT HAPPENED? and then threw it back in and waited.

The rock didn't come back next time. Something light slapped into the grass. It was a lab notebook, with an extension cord wrapped around it for weight.

WE LOST THE OTHERS. PERFECTED MACHINE. TWO WAY TRAVEL NOW POSSIBLE. NOT MUCH TIME LEFT HERE BUT REST OF GROUP NOT IN TARGET YEARS. WHERE ARE YOU?

I wrote back: SOME WORLD WE NEVER MADE, DOC. NO CHRISTIANITY. INDIANS, ARABS, VIKINGS! I LIVE IN A MUD HUT, MAKE PIPES, FIGHT AZTECS, PILE UP DIRT. EVERYBODY DYING OF PLAGUE BROUGHT BY STEAMBOAT. ALEXANDER'S LIBRARY NEVER BURNED. OVER TO YOU.

It was dark when the answer flew back. COME BACK THROUGH. WE NEED YOUR HELP, LEAKE. BACKGROUND LEVEL TOO HIGH. ALL DYING. HELP US FIND OTHERS, SEND THEM TO RIGHT TIME AS PLANNED. WEAR CIMP SUIT. WE NEED YOUR HELP.

I wrote WAIT on the lab book and sent it back.

Then I started a fire, the only one for kilometers, and stared out across the waters of the bayou.

I took a notebook from my pack, and started writing a sketchy account of my life since leaving Up There. I was on the third page when I stopped. I put down my map-marker.

I thought of the world I was from, and the one I was in. Both were dying. Maybe if I went back, I could find a world that was alive, not threatened, not falling apart, not on the way to ruin. There had to be one somewhere.

I looked at the CIMP suit. I looked at my spear. Then I looked at my watch.

I tore a piece of paper out of the notebook, wrote on it, wrapped it around another rock. I threw it into the darkly shimmering air beyond the fire, and punched the stopwatch function on the watch.

GO AWAY my note said. GO AWAY AND DIE SOMEWHERE ELSE, SOME OTHER TIME. THERE IS ENOUGH DEATH HERE ALREADY. THIS WORLD IS DYING BUT IS NOT DEAD YET. I LIKE CARVING PIPES. I LIKE FIGHTING AZTECS. GO AWAY. IN ONE HOUR AND TEN MINUTES I WILL ROLL THREE GRENADES ONE AFTER THE OTHER INTO THE TIME MACHINE. THAT'S TEN MINUTES YOUR TIME STARTING <u>NOW</u>.

In one hour and four minutes the shimmering stopped.

I could hear the pop of the fire, the croaking of frogs, the buzzing of mosquitoes. At least we don't have malaria or yellow fever yet. Maybe those are next.

I got up and kicked out the fire. I left the Army stuff where it lay, all except for the extension cord, which I can trade with the jewelry maker so he can make necklaces from it.

Toward home, then. I'll return to the new village. I will become the pipemaker. I'll marry Sunflower, if she will have me. I'll hunt and joke with the guys. Every day we'll go out and pile a little more dirt on Took-His-Time, raising the mound. Some day it will be bigger than Khoka up the River, bigger than the sky; it will go up into the air and dwarf the bluff where Natchez should be.

I'll do that because Took was my friend, and what are friends for except to pile a little more dirt on you after you're gone?

So I'll become a Moundbuilder Rotarian, and live as long as I can, and do my best, and try to make life as nice as I can for those around me.

But I still *will not* be circumcised.

Toward home, then.

"And being necessitated to eye the
remaining particle of futurity,
are naturally constituted into
thoughts of the next world,
and cannot excusably decline
the consideration of that duration,
which maketh Pyramids
pillars of snow,
and all that's past a moment."

— Browne, *Urn Burial*

"A tooth-ache deviling him, The Author took 250 drops of laudanum in a glass of Gatorade as an anodyne, and fell asleep in his chair at the moment he was reading a sentence in Henry C. Shetrone's *The Mound-Builders*. He remained in a sleep, at least of the external senses, for about three hours, during which time he has the confidence he composed no less than 5000 pages of a novel. On awaking, he appeared to have a distinct recollection of the whole, and taking down his pen, ink and paper, instantly and eagerly wrote down the lines that are here preserved. At this moment he was unfortunately called out by a person on business from Porlock, and detained by him above 14 years, and on his return to his room found to his no small surprise and mortification that, though he retained some dim remembrance of the whole, with the exception of some 225 pages of a small and difficult nature, the rest had passed away like the images on the surface of a stream into which a rock has been cast ..."

Afterword

Walk A Mile In My Moccasins

Well, it wasn't like that, but it might as well have been, and a lot of people would have been much happier. I'd been reading Amerindian history and archeology for years and years, and knew I was eventually going to write about it. (Since we're talking initial inception here, 1970, I had at that time sold one short story and exactly two articles.) *Them Bones* started, in its original altered form, the same place the *next* novel I'm writing (*I, John Mandeville*) did — with an image of a guy in early Renaissance England watching a bright meteor fall.

I thought about that a lot for five or six years, during which time I became a hotshot young turk of a writer, selling thirty or so stories and half a novel, and since the publisher of *that* had an option on whatever else of book-length either me or Buddy Saunders wrote next, I fired up a couple of chapters and an outline of something (which sorta-kinda parallels the Leake sections) called, like, *Kingdom of Death and Dreams*, or some awful thing like that.

In this original spavined form it was about a European who somehow gets to America in the late 1300s, when the Hopewell and Mississippian cultures were at their height, and who travels all over, seeing all sorts of Amerindian cultures before the coming of the horse, ends up in suspended animation in a mound, and wakes up in 1890 in time to see the end of the Plains Indians culture during the winter of the Ghost Dance and the Battle of Wounded Knee. There were all sorts of poignant stuff in there (I also remember manticores and sidehill gougers and stuff) and something like the European's tombstone: Sir Guy de Geek 1342-1371; 1889-1904.

You can imagine how *good* it was. For my troubles I got back the single most condescending rejection letter I ever got in my life, which effectively ended my association with *that* publisher.

Well, time goes by and I become even more of a hotshot writer, and all the time I'm still thinking about the moundbuilder novel, and things are falling together in my mind; a snippet of research here, an unused idea for a story Steve Utley and I never wrote, and all the time I'm working on other stuff.

Somewhere in there I realize the original stuff's only a half or a third of the book. I didn't know how I knew that, or what the other parts were, but I was sure of it. Writing is an imprecise art at best.

Meanwhile all these other publishers are bothering me for a novel. I keep saying yeah, yeah, I'll have something soon, and keep writing short stories and *not* making a living.

Then the phone rings and it's Terry Carr. He says, "I'm reviving the Ace SF Specials and I want a book from you."

Okay, Terry. I don't know about you, but growing up and trying to write in the late '60's, I always wanted to be an Ace SF Special like *Isle of the Dead* or *The Mueller-Fokker Effect*; in fact, I probably would have killed to be one.

But meanwhile two other publishers are in line for whatever book I want to write so I do a couple of new chapters (Bessie I, Leake I, I think) and an outline, and an explanation of *how* the book is to be written and put together, designed to frighten off everyone *but* Terry, and send it off to my agent, Joe Elder, and the publishers have what's known as an auction, which, to make a long story short, Terry wins.

This is early 1981 (and excuse me if my chronology for the next few years is skewed: everything I'm going to talk about happened between early '81 and late '84).

Shit. Now I've got to write a *book*. For the first time in eight years. I'm supposed to be the first book in the new Specials. (The other people in the line were to be punks not many people had heard of at the time — Lucius Shepard, Kim Stanley Robinson, Michael Swanwick, Carter Scholz, and a new kid named William Gibson.)

I waded in with all the good intentions in the world. I took out my $1.00 Schaeffer cartridge fountain pen and my two Kliban note pads I'd got for 50¢ @ and went to work. So many pages a week till it's done, so much time for research ...

About two weeks later my story "The Ugly Chickens" won the Nebula. You could have knocked me over with a feather. Okay. Things are looking up for the kid. But writers don't live in vacuums, and I was to have this lesson pounded into me again and again. It was sort of like, as the Firesign Theatre used to say, having bees live in your hat.

It had been so long since I'd written a novel that the long-haul gears were frozen and the derailleur was rusty. I'd had Buddy Saunders as collaborator in 1973 — we did do the ten pages a day first draft, ten pages a day second draft, ten pages a day third draft thing back then, finishing *The Texas-Israeli War: 1999* in 93 working days. Some say it reads like it. To those, we quote Warren Norwood's words, "Call us when you get back from 'Nam."

Well, I'd come not to work like that. I'd wait around until a story's ready, then I'd write it. Sometimes that's a few days from getting the idea, researching, to writing. Sometimes it's months. Sometimes years. (In '81 I'd been thinking of *Them Bones*, in one form or another, for 11 years.)

The other thing you find is that the longer you work on one thing, the more ideas you get on other stuff. (The Mandeville file grew by leaps and bounds when I slowed down on *Them Bones*, short story ideas kept coming to me, ones I absolutely could not ignore.)

Leigh Kennedy, with whom, in the '80's phrase, I shared my life at the time, and to whom the book is dedicated, would go to her day job at Austin Community College, come home, knock out a great story every week or two, and do a dozen other things, slowly began to wonder what I was doing all the time.

Well I was researching and writing. But it wasn't ten pages a day, or five, or two. The pile was growing, but like the snail climbing Mt. Fuji, slowly, slowly.

I was supposed to do an article for *The Writer*. (Like with the Ace SF Specials, if you'd have told me I was going to have an article in *The Writer*, I wouldn't have believed you.) Then Philip K. Dick dropped dead, after, as I understand it, having a fight with a publisher who wanted him to do a *novelization* of the screenplay of a movie based on one of his novels, instead of reissuing the novel itself, and then the people at Pocket Books tried the old Scott Meredith end-run; the field's all of a sudden going to the shit that it is today, right in front of me, and I can no longer write in good conscience to struggling young writers "SF is the wide-open field where anything goes and quality *always* wins out." anymore, so I have to write *The Writer* and say sorry, I'm not your man anymore.

"The Ugly Chickens" is up for a Hugo. Somehow, I realize that I have commitments to be Toastmaster or Guest of Honor at 14 conventions in the next two years — that's okay, I think, the book will be done *long* before then. I'm writing short stories. I finish "God's Hooks!" for Terry's *Universe 12* at Denvention, where "Ugly Chickens" loses a Hugo. It went on to win the World Fantasy Award and lose the coveted Balrog.

"Flying Saucer Rock and Roll" which was sold to Marta Randall to take the place of "Ugly Chickens" (which for complex and uninteresting reasons was first at *Universe* then at *New Dimensions* then *back* at *Universe* and which should be in *New Dimensions 13*) is suddenly an orphan, the publisher having pulled the book two weeks before publication, *after* review copies have already gone out. Now I have to sell it again.

I wrote "Ike at the Mike" because Lew Shiner and Chad Oliver wouldn't. *Them Bones* grows slowly. The advance is gone and soon I'm back down to whatever I make on short stories and what Leigh brings in from her Day Job.

Then I stop and write *The Dodo: A Scientific Romance*, about 20,000 words, using all that leftover research from "The Ugly Chickens," to enter in the Dutton Animal Book Award, for which they will pay a zillion simoleons. The contest is usually won by Boy-And-His-Marmot or Girl-And-Her-Weasel books, and here I am sending in a history of the didine birds written in dispassionate prose, with not a single scene of Boy-Having-to-Old-Yeller his sick bird ("He's your dodo, Travis. You'll have to kill it.")

Then I had to stop and write "Man-Mountain Gentian" because it and zen-sumo were keeping me from working on the book. Meanwhile I was reading, reading, reading. Quotes for the Leake chapters. Books on how you worked pipestone. I was continually amazed at how much knowledge you had to carry around if you lived in a non-literate culture. I was trying to put all that in the manuscript — I was really trying my damndest.

Then I wrote what I have come to refer to as The Story, which I'd wanted to write since I was ten years old, and sold it to The Magazine, as I have come to refer to it. Well, it's not quite right; okay, I'll do the revisions, I'm a *pro*.

Meanwhile the phone calls from Terry become a little more frequent. My book had moved from opening the Specials, to being second. Then third. Etc. No big deal. Terry was a great editor — you could always buy him off with quality.

The Story comes back. I revise it.

A month later it comes back for more revisions. I do those.

I work on *Them Bones*. We've passed the turn-in date by this time; it's okay, just do your best work, said Terry.

Back comes The Story again. More revisions. The money's been spent already. Leigh and I are fooling with the idea of building a house in the woods. (*Never* try to buy the American Dream on $5000 a year, in a good year.) I buy a pickup to haul lumber. It immediately blows up. (Later, it's towed away as an abandoned vehicle, but I get ahead of myself.) I have paid the IRS two years of back taxes. *Yo tengo no dinero*.

Terry starts calling *a lot*.

Even my agent, Joe, the calmest guy in the world, is worried.

The Story has Come Back for Another Rewrite.

I'm going crazy by this time. I'll swear I wrote the section telling what happened with the radio that I refer to in the Box section, but I didn't, did I? Maybe I dreamed it. Maybe I dreamed the whole goddam thing since I won the Nebula?

I put in the Mormon stuff (there from the first) to add verisimilitude and to cheese off Scott Card. I wrote *another* story for Mike Bishop's *Light Years and Dark* to make up for another story somebody else ended up with, and so I wouldn't be represented there with a ten-year-old story. I signed a contract for *Howard Who?*, my first short story collection.

The Story Comes Back Again. I write the mammoth scenes in *Them Bones*. I try to make sure all the distances in the Leake and Box sections are metric, in the Bessie sections in English units. I have had a toothache for more than a year.

The phone rings and rings.

The Story Comes Back. Fuck off I say I'll give you your goddamn money back I'm not working on it anymore It's done.

The phone rings and rings.

I quit answering it, just like that. Let the sonofabitch ring. I don't care. Ha ha ha ha.

A month later I turn in *Them Bones*.

Terry says it's great but you should recount your words it looks a little slim. That's strange it looked a little *fat* to me. So I put back in a section I'd taken out which I thought made the book too long (the journey upriver to the pipestone quarry.)

By now, the book's fifth on the list.

When the page proofs come, I get to read the book for the first time.

That may sound strange to you, but it's true. See, when I wrote it, I wrote it in sections. Like, Leake 15 here, The Box 12 there, Bessie 2 over here. When I thought they were done enough, I typed them up and put them in the folder. Such are our hopes and dreams that I figured if I knew what happened in every section, and each scene, and that if they all worked, the book would work.

The day I'd finished the last section to be done, I'd gone down to Kinko's, run off four copies of everything, then sat down and put them in order — Bessie 1, Leake 1, The Box 1 and so on, then hand-numbered the pages and mailed them off.

When the proofs came, I was surprised — first that it was readable — secondly that it flowed together from scene to scene just as I had planned, one working off another, resonating, as if I had written it all in order that way. Boy, am I *good*, I thought.

The other Ace Specials came out: *The Wild Shore*, *Green Eyes*, *Neuromancer* (with, as someone once said, Darth Vader's Dog on the original cover) — they sold really well, got reviewed up the wazoo. *Them Bones* came out in October 1984. You could hear it squealing like a pig as it disappeared down the chute of the American pub. biz.

In little more than two years it sold a whopping 17,000 copies in paperback, and they sent me a royalty statement with a big F for Final on it, and it goes to join all those other great books in the land of the Woodpecker God.

Or so we all thought. There's this neat Italian edition —
Scheletari nel Mississippi (*Skeletons from Beneath the
Mississippi* — truth in advertising if there ever was any),
and a German edition, and a beautiful French one,
Histoire d'Os by a publisher who has since, of course, gone
bust. Later this year there'll be a hardcover in England
from Legends, and now there's this: Mark's beautiful
edition.

What can I tell you? I knew what I was doing? So did
Terry? That without him, and Leigh, there'd be no
Them Bones, that I'd probably still be talking about writing
it, 18 years later?

Well, it was grief Terry sure didn't need at the time; me
either, for sure. But now I'm able to look on the whole
three years and the book as Character-Building and Good
For The Soul.

You know I wouldn't have had it *any* other way.

Howard Waldrop
November 22, 1988